Juhani Aho

Squire Hellman and Other Stories

Juhani Aho

Squire Hellman and Other Stories

ISBN/EAN: 9783744751414

Printed in Europe, USA, Canada, Australia, Japan

Cover: Foto ©Andreas Hilbeck / pixelio.de

More available books at **www.hansebooks.com**

SQUIRE HELLMAN

AND

OTHER STORIES

PSEUDONYM LIBRARY

JUHANI AHO

———

SQUIRE HELLMAN

AND

OTHER STORIES

LONDON

T. FISHER UNWIN

PATERNOSTER SQUARE

—

M DCCC XCIII

CONTENTS.

INTRODUCTION.

THE FINNISH NOVEL.

THE Finnish novel may be called the baby of the great Romance Family. Thirty years [1] ago it was unborn, but from the very first hour of its birth it displayed an astonishing vitality and shot up so swiftly in every direction as to leave very little room in the native literature for anything else. It is true that we do find a few somewhat second-

---

[1] I do not forget Gummerus and Kivi; but they can scarcely be taken seriously as romance-writers. They were rather pioneers who cleared the way for a later generation. The Finnish novel really begins with *Päivärinta*.

rate lyric poets among the modern
native writers, while *Minna Canth*
has shown that the language of
the Kalevala can even lend itself
to the requirements of the modern
drama ; but, taken as a whole,
the Finnish literature is a literature
of novels. That this literature has
hitherto entirely escaped the notice
of foreign scholars is scarcely sur-
prising when one considers the
comparative isolation of the Finnish
people and the superlative difficulty
of the Finnish language ; but that
it will become known, one day, may
be fairly assumed in an age so
greedy of discoveries and so curious
of novelties as our own. In the
meantime, a brief description of this
out-of-the-way corner of the Repub-
lic of Letters may, perhaps, serve as
an introduction to the *first* English
translation of a Finnish novel.

The most characteristic and
original of the Finnish novelists is
Pietari Päivärinta. Born in 1827
of parents so poor that they were
frequently forced to send out their
children to beg bread for the
starving family, he followed the
plough till comparatively late in
life when an accident laid him, for
a time, on a bed of sickness. From

his boyish days he had always
hungered after knowledge and
devoured, in his rare moments of
leisure, such books as fell in his
way, and he now employed his
enforced leisure in writing a description of his own simple but
bitter experiences, entitled " Elä-
mänä " (My life). This little sketch
(it consists of but sixty-two pages)
was, in 1876, published by the
National Finnish Educational
Society, and met with a success
which justified the author in
quitting agriculture for literature.
He now began that long series of
novels and sketches which have
made his name so famous in his
native land, and of which the
following are the most notable :
" Elämän havannoita " (Reflections
from life) ; " Minä ja muut " (Myself and others) ; " Uudistalo "
(The new settlement) ; " Halla
aamuna " (A frosty morning) ;
"Vaimoni " (My wife) ; " Tahdon
voima " (The power of the will),
the two latter being especially
beautiful and pathetic stories.
Päivärinta is the chronicler *par
excellence* of Finnish peasant-life ;
but his method, though simple, is
peculiar. He is perhaps best de-

scribed as a religious realist. He
excels in analysis of character, and
his analysis is minute and searching,
flinching from no detail which can
give point or finish to his narrative.
He describes the drunkenness and
other vices of the peasantry with a
vividness born of actual experience ;
but a moral, a religious purpose
lies at the bottom of all his realism.
A pietist himself, his belief in the
authority of religion, the warnings
of conscience and the radical dis-
tinction between right and wrong
are unshakable and some of his
finest tales are those in which the
human soul is shown struggling in
the grip of some tyrannous vice
from which it escapes indeed, but
never scatheless. Two other most
amiable characteristics of *Päivärinta*
are his intense fellow-feeling for the
neglected and the oppressed and a
subtle appreciation of all that is
best and noblest in womankind.
In his longer and later works,
however, his moralising is ex-
cessive, his characters sometimes
sink to the level of idealised
abstractions and his most whole-
some reflections would frequently
be none the worse for a little
humorous seasoning.

Next to *Päivärinta*, decidedly
the most original of the Finnish
novelists, is *Juho Reijonen*, also a
man of the people and parish priest
in his native place ; but while the
sexton [1] is never so great as when
he is serious, the parson is nothing
if not gay. *Reijonen*, in fact, is a
genial optimist who takes life good-
naturedly and looks upon the world
with an indulgent eye. His shorter
stories, such, for instance, as " Syn-
keän Matin juttu " (The tale of
gloomy Matthew), in his " Uusia
Kertoelmia " (Later sketches), are
exquisite miniatures drawn with
characteristically Finnish elabora-
tion of detail and bubbling over
with the sweetest, sunniest, humour.
He is less successful with the novel
or romance, his more ambitious
efforts—*e.g.*, " Vaihdokas " (The
changeling) ; " Tuuli vaaralaiset "
(In stress of weather), &c.—though
not without talent, being full of
improbabilities and extravagances
and showing both a want of constructive skill and a feebleness of
characterisation. In his studies of
child-life, however, *Reijonen* is

---

[1] *Päivärinta* was, for a long time, sexton
in his native place.

almost unsurpassable, falling not very far short, in this respect, of Hans Christian Andersen himself.

The study of child-life, however, seems to be a speciality of the Finnish novelists, and the literature abounds with beautiful little tales of this kind. Thus, to take only a couple of instances, *Kauppis-Heikki* in " Aiden Kuoltua " (After mother's death), has written a comically pathetic sketch of how Spinning Peggy foretells, from the cards, the fate of a little girl who has just been left motherless, the child herself being the narrator, while *Lissa Tervo*, a labourer's wife, describes in " Uusi isä " (The new father), how a little fatherless girl hears that she has got " a new papa " while on a visit to her aunt. All the way home the child's fancy conjures up visions of her old papa coming back to her from heaven in glorified raiment, only to find, at her journey's end, a hard, exacting step-father who speedily puts to flight her innocent illusions. This pretty little story rightly obtained a place of honour in the well-known (in Finland) collection of popular sketches published by *Söderström* and entitled " Syvistä reveistä " (From the lowest ranks).

Stories relating to religious and educational subjects seem to have an especial attraction for the rising school of Finnish novelists. The gifted lady who writes under the pseudonym of *Kyösti* gives a powerful description of the curious pietistic sect known as the Hihhuli grounded on personal experience. Another puritan sect called Körtil-laiset,[1] is vigorously attacked in a novel of rude power, extraordinarily rich in proverbs, entitled " Korpelan Tapani " (Our way of going on at Korpela). The author, *Heikki Meri-läinen*, is a blacksmith of Korpela.

Prominent among the novelists with a purpose is *Minna Canth* who made her *début* a short time ago as a popular dramatist of considerable merit. Her novels, how ever, have by no means increased her reputation. The wrongs of her sex, real and imaginary, is her constant theme, and she is never weary—especially in " Salakari " (Breakers)—of dwelling on the sufferings of poor weak woman at the hands of her natural tyrant and oppressor man. Exaggeration and a hopeless pessimism characterise

---

[1] *Lit.*, Shirt-walkers.

these vigorous but dismal and unpleasant stories.

An author of a very different
calibre is the lady already alluded
to under the soubriquet of *Kyösti*,
who has produced one of the most
striking novels in the literature,
" Räisäs-poika " (Räisänén's son).
The motive of this tale is somewhat
similar to Jonas Lie's well-known
masterpiece : " Livsslaven." It is
the sad story of a poor little outcast
lad, the son of thievish parents,
whose early life is pretty equally
divided between the wilderness and
the jail, and whose heroic upward
struggle against all but overwhelm-
ing difficulties are most pathetically
described. *Kauppis-Heikki*, who
has also been mentioned before as
a student of child-life, has not sus-
tained the promise of his earlier
works which show genuine humour
and considerable descriptive power.
His later works are dull, commonplace, and somewhat coarse. *Ka-
simir Leino*, on the other hand,
himself an eminent critic, has
written in " Emmalan Elli " a
work of real genius. The heroine
is a poor peasant " love-child " who
is never able to get the better of
the stigma with which she first

entered the world. To avoid the
killing scorn of her birthplace, she
emigrates to town, becomes a
factory-girl, and for some time
manages to keep her head above
water till, wearied out by the
flaunts and gibes of her companions
who ridicule her quiet, simple ways,
she seeks protection in the friend-
ship of her master's son who
betrays and then abandons her to
misery and, ultimately, madness.
Another rising young author is
Santeri Ingman whose humorously
sarcastic novel " Hellaassa " (In
Hellas) produced a great sensation.
Hellas is a restaurant near the
capital where the hero, Eljas, a
romantic young student, makes the
acquaintance of a pretty waitress
whom he resolves to " save " by
marrying her. Till he is ready to
offer her a home, however, the
young lovers solemnly agree that
their affection shall be purely
platonic, not so much as a kiss
being allowed to pass between
them. The irony of fate, however,
brings them together one Christ-
mas Eve under circumstances which
drive all their stoical resolutions
to the winds. The girl suffers for
both, as usual, while Eljas, quitting

romance for reality, blossoms into a radical reformer and organises a crusade against society, till an unexpected legacy converts him to more conservative views. Finally he settles down as a curate, marries the daughter of his vicar, and accepts a quiet country life, which flows along like a dream, as the ideal lot of man. In a later volume of sketches—" Ilta puhteeksi " (Before Dusk)—Ingman has also approved himself a master of style and a humorist of the first rank. Many of these sketches are irresistibly funny.

But the Prince of the Finnish novelists, whom I have reserved last of all for separate consideration because his genius so widely separates him from the rest of his fellow-craftsmen, is the pseudonymous *Juhani Aho*, the son of the parish priest of Iderisalmi, whose literary career only began some twelve years ago, but who must already be recognised as one of the leading novelists of the North. *Aho's* art combines all the photographic exactness and all the generous sensitiveness of *Päivärinta* with a humour as genuine but far broader and deeper than the humour of

Reijonen, and he possesses, besides,
a graceful fancy and a vivid imagination—qualities, by the way, in
which Finnish novelists are generally somewhat deficient. He is
also by far the most cultured of
Finnish writers. He has studied
to advantage the masterpieces of
Scandinavian literature, and in his
later novels one detects the influence
of the modern French school whose
leading representatives are Paul
Bourget and Édouard Rod. But
Aho's own genius is far too original
and independent to seek for inspiration outside itself, though, no
doubt, he owes something of his
exquisitely finished style to the
patient care with which he has
studied the best foreign models.
The most important of his earlier
works is " Rautatie " (The Railway), in which, with genuine
Finnish humour and circumstan-
tiality he describes the effect the
first sight of a railway has upon
an old peasant couple who won't
believe in it till they've seen it and
don't approve of it when they have.
Some Finnish critics still think that
" Rautatie " is *Aho's* best story, and
the constructive ability with which
a novel of more than one hundred

pages is made out of next to nothing is truly amazing ; but English readers, at any rate, would find it a trifle too long ; and the same remark applies to a later novel, " Muuan Markkamies " (A market man). Of the deepest psychological interest, on the other hand, is " Papin Tytär " (The Priest's daughter), a pathetic story of a highly gifted young girl whose efforts to educate herself above the dead level of her commonplace surroundings are snubbed and thwarted by ignorant and narrow-minded parents. Finally, the girl is forced to sacrifice her youthful ideals for the sake of a husband whom she can neither love nor respect. A story of equal power, but as broadly humorous as " Papin Tytär " is melancholy, is " Hellmanin Herra " (Squire Hellman), written in 1887, which gives its name to the present volume, and must therefore be left to speak for itself. " Hellmanin Herra " was quickly followed by " Helsinkiin," an undoubtedly vigorous, but decidedly repulsive description of student orgies, the central figure of which is a weak young reprobate who is preyed upon and corrupted by other young sinners more wicked than himself. This book produced a painful impression upon a large section of the Finnish public and was the beginning of a sharp polemic between the author's critics, who accused him of realism, and his admirers who justified his new departure.

In 1890 *Aho* visited Paris at the expense of the State, and on his return published two fresh works of indisputable genius, " Yksin " (Lonely), a novel, and "Lastuja" (Splinters), a collection of tales and sketches. These works revived the warfare between the realists and the anti-realists. The former hailed them as the most perfect manifestations of the author's peculiar talent, especially praising in them that combination of sound realism and noble, passionless idealism which, they maintain, is to be found in no other Northern novelist ; while the anti-realists bitterly complained that the author of " Hellmanin Herra " had deliberately chosen the downward path and that he had requited the liberality of his country in sending him abroad by bringing back to her not bread but a stone. "Yksin" is a powerful psychological study of the effect of rejected advances on a *blasé* man of the world who discovers, to his own surprise, that he has still a heart. There are some wonderful descriptions in it, but little humour and less plot. As to "Lastuja," I can only say that it is a string of gems of style of the purest water, and certainly contains nothing which English taste should consider objectionable. I have selected two of the tales contained in it (*i.e.*, "Pioneers" and "Loyal") to make up the present volume, adding, besides, the much earlier and charming sketch, "When Father brought home the Lamp," which shows *Aho* in his first simplicity.

The future progress of *Aho* must be looked forward to with intense interest by all lovers of literature. That he has, to some extent, thrown in his lot with the realists seems pretty evident ; but the genuine humour, graceful fancy, tender melancholy, and intense feeling which are his peculiar characteristics, seem to indicate a soul above the gutter of so-called *naturalism*.

R. NISBET BAIN.
Editor and Translator.

November, 1892.

SQUIRE HELLMAN.

FROM THE FINNISH OF JUHANI AHO.

I.

THE whole house was topsy-turvy, for the squire was about to go out. He was again in a horribly bad temper, bawled upstairs and downstairs, and rounded furiously upon his wife and the maids, who rushed about terror-stricken to obey his orders and only got in each other's way.

"Why is my shaving-water so hot that it has to stand and cool for hours together before a man can dip his chin in it? Why is it, I say—why? Who was it that heated it? Hie! Where the deuce have

they all got to ? " he roared, till all
the windows rattled.

The squire was shaving himself
in his own room and thought that
his wife was in the adjoining
chamber. But, as he got no answer,
he rushed out, like a lunatic, to look
for her in the inner apartments.
He had got no further than the
threshold when his wife came
bounding up from the kitchen.

" Why is this water here so hot ?
Do you want me to be boiled like
pork ? What do you mean by it,
eh ? "

" It's that Anni—but I'll go at
once and . . ." mumbled his wife,
and went straightway off to the
kitchen for some cold water.

" Why has Anni made the
squire's shaving-water too hot ?
Haven't I told you time after
time . . ."

" I'm sure it was no hotter than
usual."

" It's always the same story," said
the flurried wife ; " but go now and
fetch some cold . . . the squire is
wild . . . and go and fetch the
squire's pelisse from the hall and
warm it before the fire." And the
lady herself dashed off to the
squire's room with the cold water

and began to pour a little of it into the washing-basin.

"What—what the dickens are you doing there?"

"I am pouring in a little cold water."

"Yes, of course, and you go and make it so cold that one's skin regularly freezes. Is a man *always* to put up with this sort of thing? It is always like this when one has to go anywhere. The whole lot of them like born idiots! Put the can on the drawers, can't you! Do you mean to hold it in your hand all day long? And why couldn't you have gone and fetched it yourself at first, I should like to know?"

"I was in the pantry, and I said to Anni . . ."

"Although I've told you a hundred times that she doesn't know how to prepare shaving-water and that you oughtn't to let her do it."

"And I wouldn't have done it either, but when I heard you were going to town, I thought of sending to the sexton's wife a little meat against the festival in return for the socks she has knitted."

"I haven't any room for your

bundle . . . she must come and
fetch it herself."

"But she has no horse of her
own, you know."

"Then she must take the hand-
sledge. Well, dash the water in
there! So! And where's the
towel?"

"I have it here."

"Give it me then, can't you?
Have you told them to inspan?"

"I haven't yet . . . but I'll do
so at once."

And away skipped the wife to
tell them. She had to go right to
the very stables before she could
find the stable-boy. She was quite
in an agony, poor wretch! for fear
she shouldn't come across him.
Her shoulders were stooping and
her figure quite bent double, as,
with unsteady steps, she flopped
across the yard to the stable and
from the stable back to the house
again.

"What an ugly old fool it is!"
growled the squire, as he stood at
the window and watched her.

He had settled down to shaving,
but he was in a terrible hurry all
along, and hissed through his
grinding teeth—

. "And to have to shave oneself,

too! For such gentry as they, forsooth! I should do much better if I went unshaved as I am. In night-dresses and slippers too! A pretty thing! There they sit and tax other men's property! Beggarly rats, the whole lot of them! But they know how to flay other people, anyhow! However, we shall just see who's the master here!"

The fact of the matter was, the court of assessors was in session in the vestry-hall to assess the amount of taxes all the people should pay. And thither, too, the squire was about to repair to look after his interests, for he had heard . . .

"Hie!" he roared, suddenly, so that a large piece of whitewash fell down from the ceiling.

He was just about to rise from his seat when his wife came rushing in again.

"Have you all lost your hearing? Did Pulkkinen come hither? . . . isn't he sitting in the back room?"

"I fancy so. I'll go at once . . ."

In a few moments Pulkkinen himself came in through the front room door.

"Now, listen to me! What was it they said? No lies, mind!"

"I ain't lying. It's perfectly true; I heard them say it with my own ears. I was in the hall at the time, and made it a point to remember everything they said in the room within."

"Well, well! what was it they said? Say exactly what you heard them say!"

"I can't recollect it word for word, nor did I hear it all, but it seemed to be their opinion that . . ."

"Which of them was it who said so?"

"They all said it."

"Did the bailiff say so too?"

"Like enough, but I did not exactly hear."

"You did hear—you heard well enough, though you won't say; . . . you are a big blockhead. . . ."

"I assure you, Squire, it was so."

"And they said, did they, that Squire Hellman should be taxed right stiffly, eh?"

"That's what they said."

"And what else? Come, now! That he is rich and ought to be regularly plucked? Out with it."

"Yes; and that the tax should

be assessed on an income of 6,000 marks at the least. That's what they threatened."

The squire's eyes sparkled at the mirror like the eyes of a savage dog.

" For six thou ...! I'll show the rascals that. . . . And I'll let them see that if I lose the whole d—d thing by it, I'll . . . Hie, there ! Hie ! "

The servant girl rushed into the room as quickly as if she had been kicked in.

" Why can't you come quicker when I call you ? Take away the shaving-water and bring in washing-water ! Why can't your mistress come herself ? "

" She wasn't there ! "

" Then where was she ? "

" She's in the kitchen holding squire's pelisse before the fire."

" Six thousand ! It is scandalous, swineish ; it is a downright Shylock way of going to work ! Am I, forsooth, to pay the whole of the taxes of the parish ? Hey ? "

" There were some who seemed to think that it might even be appraised at 10,000 marks."

" Hey—hey ? "

" Yes ; and that if the timber

business showed a good profit—
they take a note of every blessed
thing, you see—what business is it
of theirs ?"

Even while he was saying this
Pulkkinen fancied that the squire
would flog him into tatters and flay
him alive. So he took his pre-
cautions before he named the
10,000 and gripped the door-latch.

But the squire said never a word.
He only became a little paler, the
veins on his temples swelled and
grew blue, his nostrils extended as
if they were about to fly apart, and
his mouth had a nasty twitch two
or three times running.

The same moment, the maid
brought the washing-water.

"Is the horse already fore-
spanned ?"

"Not yet, I think ; . . . the boy
asked if he should come and drive."

"Let him wait till he's asked !
Well, let him come ! And tell him
to tie the bell to the thill, and take
the embossed bit and harness.
We'll drive in state to-day !
There'll be no begging for mercy
here ! We'll show the devils
something. You come too, Pulkkinen ! "

"All right ! "

His wife brought him his pelisse. Turning his back towards her the squire swung it over his shoulders, and without so much as a " Thank you ! " fumbled for the belt. His wife found it for him.

" Shall I fasten it behind ? "

" Be off ! "

And without saying adieu, he went into the yard with his whip in his hand, which always hung on a nail in the outer room. His wife felt that she really could breathe more easily when the door was slammed to. Luckily his wrath had, this time, not burst forth against her, but the wife thought she knew her husband well enough to foresee that it would not be very long before it did. She was afraid, but, for all that, she went to the window to peep out from behind the curtains.

The horse was standing in front of the steps, the rug was spread out as the squire liked it, and the stable-boy held the reins in order to give them to the squire as soon as he had taken his seat. Before he sat down, however, the squire examined everything pretty narrowly, looked to see if the bell was properly fastened to the thill and tested the saddle-straps to see how tightly they were drawn. Everything was in such order that he could find no fault at all. His wife already began to hope that he might, after all, set off without flying into a rage.

"Oh, that young horse, I only hope he won't beat it. . . . Heaven be merciful to us, . . . if he isn't safely off at last!"

When the squire took his seat in the sledge, the horse started off a little too soon, and when the reins were pulled in, it began to back. Then it got one or two flicks with the whip and started forward. But as the reins kept on tugging and the whip whizzing, it reared first on one leg and then on the other, and then rushed off at full gallop, so that the sledge was bumped against the door-post.

Then it was taken out and led to the stable.

"Alas! alas! now it will be flogged again," moaned the wife, and she hastened out into the yard in front of the kitchen. There the maids were standing already and looking about them with frightened faces, yet out they always would go to listen, whenever master flogged his horses,

From time to time one heard from the stable the squire's angry cries, the slashing of the whip-cord, and the trampling of horses' feet. The terrified lad stood in front of the stable without knowing what to do with himself. But when the squire had had enough of it, and brought the trembling horse out into the yard, the boy very narrowly escaped having something for himself too.

"What are you standing gaping for here with your tail between your legs, eh? Drag the sledge here, or you'll taste the butt-end of my whip!" roared the squire.

The wife and the maids had vanished in a twinkling from the front door, for the squire couldn't bear any one to stand and listen while he "coached" his horses.

Trembling all over, but without otherwise moving a limb, the horse allowed itself to be inspanned.

"Skip up on to the rocker, Pulk-kinen!" cried the squire from the door. Pulkkinen had been standing there and filling his pipe while he waited. "And you try now and drive if you can!" growled he at the boy, who had sprung up on the coach-box. And he gave the reins to him.

But the uproar in the yard and in the stable had been overheard by the neighbours, and all who were astir there had stopped to listen.

" To-day there are no magpies to sit and laugh on the roof of the manor-house," said some one.

" What could have put up his back so ! " asked another.

" It doesn't take very much to do that ; . . . perhaps a twig fell down across his path."

" His horse got just such a basting yesterday because it didn't turn into the stable quick enough to please him. Yes, first he flogged that horse, and then he flogged all the other horses—the stallions, the bood-mare, and even the old horse that draws the water. Last of all the stable-boy had him about his ears . . ."

" Come, come ! "

" I tell you it's true. He went talking about it himself."

" Did the boy want to stop him ? "

" Yes, of course he did."

" Well, opposition like that makes him bite like a wolf ; . . . but his wife suffers terribly, they say. It is at her that he swears and thunders the most."

" But how about the maids ? "

"Yes, he rounds upon them too."

Such was the almost daily criticism of the neighbours on the conduct of Squire Hellman.

";But can't they try and get him bound over to keep the peace ? "

" He has never been bound over yet, . . . but if it goes on like this . . . "

" It would do him a world of good, and then, perhaps, he would behave himself a little better."

"There is no security that he will ever behave himself a little better. . . ."

II.

THE tax-assessors were sitting in the vestry-hall and appraising the people's property. The table stood right in front of the window through which one could survey the broad acres of the parsonage, and, behind the broad acres, the church. At one end of the table, verifying the registers, sat the president of the Board—an ex-captain of reserves, but now a landed proprietor, with spectacles on nose and a pen in his mouth. Right opposite to him sat

3

the bailiff.[1]   He sat there on behalf
of the Crown, with his back against
the wall and his right elbow leaning
on the table while his hand sup-
ported his pipe ; for amongst such
close acquaintances smoking was
not forbidden even in the official
chamber.   Some of them were
smoking, others were leisurely
leaning forward, and spat from time
to time between their knees.   One
or two did not even do that, but
merely sat there and peeped from
time to time out of the window into
the courtyard where the crowd kept
up an uninterrupted gabble.   One
of them, for comfort's sake, had
scrambled to the top of the sexton's
lofty bed, and as he sank deeper
and deeper down, the mattress and
the dirty pillows swelled higher and
higher on both sides of him up
towards the ceiling.

" And so we come to Hukkanen,"
said the chairman, as he turned the
leaf over.   " Last year he was set
down at 250. . . . Shall we put him
down at the same figure now ? "

" We may as well, I think," said
one of the assessors, without raising
his head, and expectorating between
his knees.

---

[1] Vallesmanni.

"The alderman of Kaarnajärvi comes next. . . . No. 5. . . . Is he here in person?"

"Scarcely, I think."

"He was put down at 500 last year."

"We may charge him the same thing now."

"Very well."

"Cotter Pehkonen from the same estate."

"He's here. . . . I saw him come driving up just now," said one who was sitting and looking out of the window.

"Isn't that his horse standing by the courtyard palings?" said the one who was sitting on the bed with outstretched neck.

"Bridge-inspector, bring him in!"

"The bridge-inspector seems to have gone out," said the bailiff. "Let some one else go out and tell Pehkonen to come in."

One of the assessors took it upon him to do so.

"At what figure does Pehkonen value his taxable property this year?" said the chairman, when Pehkonen had come in and saluted them all. "It was 100 last year."

"It is really worth just nothing at all; . . . couldn't it be remitted this time just for once?" said the cotter, scratching himself behind the ear.

But the bailiff and several of the assessors protested against this forthwith.

" Remitted, say you ? Who, then, should be taxed if you are exempted—you, forsooth, who actually lend out money ? "

" Lend out, indeed ! I should very much like to know where I could find the money."

" Come, Pehkonen, none of that. Why, everybody knows about it ! " said one of the assessors.

" It wouldn't be a bit too much if we put you down at 300 marks," observed the bailiff.

" Three hundred marks ! My good sirs ! "

" Well, 300 is perhaps too much, but we may say 200 very well. Perhaps that would be fairer," opined the chairman. " Are you all agreed ? "

" Yes, all—all."

" 'Tis a deal too much," grumbled Pehkonen, as he left the room.

" And now," said the chairman, as he laughed a little and pushed his spectacles back on to his forehead— " now we come to Squire Hellman ! "

" Have we come to him already ? "

" Well, now, how much shall we assess him at ? " he asked, with peculiar emphasis. "Nobody has any idea how rich that man really is. You recollect what we said about it this morning?"

"We know this much," said the bailiff, as he went up to the stove to knock the ashes out of his pipe, " that it would not be any too much if we set him down at a higher figure than anybody else."

"But we must seriously consider the matter, so that there may be no mistake about it," said the chair- man, as he lit his pipe.

Then there was a little break in the business of the day, and the question was adjourned, or, rather, they kept to that subject alone, for a desultory conversation now arose about the means of Squire Hellman, and more particularly how he had come by them. It was very well known that he was not so badly off even when he had first come to the place from East Bothnia, and had purchased the Hovi property, which had fallen into chancery. Immedi- ately after that, he had taken unto himself a wife from his own parts, and was said to have got a pretty pot of money with her also, with

which he had set to work and
improved his property. . But his
wife had died a few years afterwards
of consumption. . . . " And I should
like to know who wouldn't have
died in the clutches of such a
venomous, black - snouted, coarse-
limbed, violent . . ."

" Come, come, I think we've
chattered about it quite enough,"
said the chairman, by way of gentle
reprimand to that particular assessor
who had let fall these epithets.

"Oh ! very well. . . . It's no
business of mine, but if one must
open one's mouth on the subject . . ."

" Has he not turned a penny or
two in the horse trade also ? " asked
the chairman, as if to cancel his
own reprimand.

" That he has. But most of his
money was made by buying up
grain. In good years he buys at a
low price, and in bad years he sells
again at double and more than
double what he paid."

" Yes, and how he snapped his
fingers and joked about it quite
lately ! ' I made a regular busting
profit by it,' said he. Why, he
gained more than 10 marks per
bushel."

"He grabs all he can, even from his own cottagers. On his lands nobody can get his rights. Only a few years ago his tenant, poor Aappo, had to sacrifice his horses, his corn, everything, in order to pay his rent and do his stipulated service."

"Wasn't he the man who was not allowed to go and cut his own rye, beg as he might, when he saw that the frost was coming?"

"Yes, it was poor Aappo Huttunen. The fellow is now a farm labourer, and his family goes about and starves."

"That's the way Hellman piles up his wealth."

"Yes, and then, too, he is so horribly stingy. Why, they say he even counts the small white fishes he gives his people to eat, and sour enough they are, too. And as for a bit of butter, it's a thing absolutely unheard of there."

The same moment a sledge-bell was heard furiously tinkling outside, and some one was seen driving past the window in hot haste.

"Why, if there isn't the fellow himself!" cried one of those who sat by the window, and they all made a rush for it and looked out.

Even the chairman stretched forward his head a little, though he
did not rise from his place as the
gentleman sitting on the bed did,
thereby dragging half the bedclothes on to the floor, for he
hadn't time to pick them up until
he had looked his fill.

"There we have him!"

"He has driven the horse till it
is dripping wet."

"And the coachman also, he has
quite . . ."

"If you take your places, gentlemen, we will go on with our
business," exhorted the captain,
suddenly, in his most official tone.
"Since the person in question has
himself arrived, and precise information is wanting as to the value
of his taxable property, it would be
best, I think, to call him up, so that
he may have the opportunity, if he
desires it, of rendering to the Board
a statement of his sources of income.
Go, bridge-inspector, and ask Squire
Hellman in."

But Hellman didn't wait to be
called. He nearly tore the door off
its hinges, and came into the room
with his pelisse on.

"Good-day," said he. His tone
was curt and truculent.

The chairman bowed stiffly from his place at the head of the table, and busily turned over his papers. The other assessors gave no sign of life whatever. Squire Hellman loosened the belt of his pelisse and glanced angrily from one to the other.

" I'll take a seat, though nobody asks me to ! " he growled in an undertone, and sat down on a vacant seat in front of the stove, first of all taking off his pelisse and pitching it on the bed. Nobody uttered a word. The only audible sound was the rustling of the chairman's papers. After turning them over for some time the chairman said at last :

" We were settling about Cotter Pehkonen from Kaarnajärvi ; his income was estimated at 200 marks."

" Yes, so it was."

" Two hundred is altogether too little," said Hellman, rising up with an air of authority. " The fellow ought to pay on much more. I know that in ready money alone his income is more than 400."

" Permit me to call your attention to the fact that the affair has already been settled, and that only the members of the Board have a voice here."

Hellman was a trifle embarrassed, but tried to hide his embarrassment by scowling on all around him. He tried his utmost to give his mouth a contemptuous twist, and shifted his quid of tobacco from one cheek to the other. There he stood with his legs stretched out to their widest, and stroked his black bushy beard incessantly.

Again the chairman was busy about his papers for such a long time that Hellman at last lost patience.

"Will there ever be an end of all this rummaging of papers?" he asked.

At last the chairman calmly raised his eyes.

"Owner of lot No. 6 at Kaarna-järvi, Squire Hellman!"

"So-ho! You've hit upon it at last, then!"

"At the last tax-assessment, according to his own estimate, his taxable income was calculated at 1,000 marks.

"It was."

"As the person immediately concerned is actually present . . ."

"Quite right; I *am* present."

". . . I venture to inquire, in the name of the Board, at what figure

Squire Hellman estimates his income
for the current year ?"

"It may stand the same as before,
though it hasn't turned out so
much."

A disgusted and unanimous
"Fie !" proceeded from the chairman and the Board.

"What !" hissed Hellman, and
they saw how the blood rushed to
his head at once.

"Mr. Chairman," said the bailiff,
"I object to that estimate as being
much too low."

"What's that ? Too low !" And
Squire Hellman quickly freed his
mouth from the quid of tobacco,
which he spat right away upon the
floor.

"Everybody knows that it's too
low. All the members of the Board
can say the same thing."

"It *is* too low," and they con-
firmed the chairman's statement
with one voice.

"How the mischief can you ? . . .
Harkye, Botberg, how the mischief
do you know my resources ? I suppose you've counted up all my
cash, eh ?"

"I may not have counted it, but
I know what it comes to all the
same — not, perhaps, exactly to a

penny, but I know it, nevertheless.
Your timber speculations are very
well known indeed, and your deal-
ings in grain, and your inherited
property, too ; . . . every one knows
about it without requiring to reckon
up your money—every one, especially
those from whom you have bought
forests to sell them to other people.
You have bragged about it yourself
before us all . . . before me and many
others, but most recently before me.”

"When did I ever boast before
you ? Don't tell lies ! I've boasted
to nobody ! ”

"You *have* boasted ; and even if
you hadn't, one has only got to
look at your new plantations and
other works to see how you're
getting on.”

"Am I to be taxed, forsooth, for
improving my property ? Am I to
be taxed for that ? Hey ? ”

"We can see what you've got,
anyhow. And you've money in
the funds and inherited property,
too.”

"Do you mean to tell me that I
am to be over-taxed because I culti-
vate my fields and invest my money
in land ? ”

"You got 10,000 marks last winter
for the woods of Honkakanga, and

I am sure all that money hasn't gone in land—now, has it?"

"If it hasn't gone in land, at any rate . . ."

"Don't you be so smart, Juntunen ; that's my business. You're not a whit wiser than other folks, although you are an assessor."

"No personalities, please!" observed the chairman, severely. "The only information we desire from Squire Hellman is, at what figure does he reckon his this year's income?"

"At just what I have already told you."

"Perhaps you will be so good as to step out of the room for a moment. If you wish to hear the resolution of the Board you may return shortly."

"All I say is that if you tax me too high . . ."

"Oh, it sha'n't be too high," said the chairman, with a laugh ; and as Hellman shut the door he heard a most irritating burst of laughter behind it.

By way of rejoinder he slammed the door after him so violently that the window rattled.

What had passed in the room within had only heightened his ill-humour.

" What sort of people do you call those fellows in there ? " cried he, violently, to those who were waiting in the hall outside. " Who has given them the right to sit there and count other people's money ? Who, I say ? Does anybody know who ? "

" Isn't it the Vestry Board that has elected them ? " said some one.

" The cat has elected them. And they are big rogues, the whole lot of them—Crown-rats, I call them. And such fellows sit upon the committee ! Rogues that haven't got a scurvy penny to bless themselves with ! "

" Why didn't they elect you, Squire, eh ? "

" Hey ? Hold your jaw, will you ? What have you got to say ? "

" A-ho ! "

" I didn't speak to you, so you have no business to speak to me. And hold your tongue ! Mind that ! "

" I'll take good care of that, but . . ."

" Do they want to tax you too high, sir ? " asked another out of the crowd.

" What's that to do with you ? "

"What, indeed!"

"Tie the halter shorter, Olli!" roared he to his stable-boy, from the top of the steps. "Haven't you learnt to tie a horse yet?"

"Who-a—so! What are you shying like that for? Who-a—so! I say."

But the timid horse feared that voice more than the whining of a whip, and only tried all the more to squeeze up against the wall as far as the short halter would allow it. And it strained itself still more violently when it saw Hellman go to the sledge and take out his whip from thence.

"I'll teach you!" he hissed, and the same instant the whipcord cut through the air and struck the beast's delicate chest. Every time the horse saw the whip raised, it tried to rise on two legs against the wall; but when the stroke fell, it stood motionless between the shafts, and trembled all over till the whip was again raised, when it again tried to avoid the blow in the same way.

The hall door was packed full of onlookers, but as they were joined by others from within, the foremost pressed their way out and assembled around Hellman. This irritated

him, and he flogged his horse all
the worse.

"It is bruising its knees against
the wall," the stable-boy ventured
to remark.

"Hold your tongue, unless you
would like to have a taste of it too.
Who-a — so ! I say. Whoa —
who-a !"

Only when the horse had quite
ceased to rear, did he lay the whip
back into the sledge. But he
looked at the horse all the same
with flaming eyes, and curbed it
with his look. But save for an
involuntary shivering, the horse
didn't stir. It had arched its head
against the wall, and followed the
least motion of its master with
shy terror in its every look.

"So, so ! You won't do that
again ! . . . " said he, as if he were
addressing a birched child. But
immediately afterwards he turned
round upon his heels towards the
crowd, and cried, "What are you
standing staring there for, you
blockheads ? Have you never seen
a horse taught before ? Be off with
you !"

The people drew back a little,
and the same moment the bridge-
inspector called him in again.

His wrath had not half-exhausted itself yet. There was a whistling in his head, the corners of his mouth were twitching, a dark shadow lay across his eyebrows, and the hair on the nape of his neck rose a little beneath his hat.

"Well ; what have *the gentlemen* to say ?" he half yelled, as he came in and stood bolt upright in the middle of the floor.

The chairman quietly gave him to understand that "inasmuch as the Board has been informed, on the best authority, that the owner of lot No. 6 at Kaarnajärvi, Squire A. Hellman, during the year last past, in consequence of various businesses and speculations, as well known to him as to the Board, has increased his means so much that the tax at which he is at present assessed ought, justly, to be raised considerably higher ; therefore the Board has considered it its duty to appraise his taxable estate at 7,000 marks. . . ."

"It's a wicked lie ! . . ."

"Which the person immediately concerned is herewith . . ."

"It is a lie of Satan's, I say, and the whole lot of you are big rogues and highway robbers—the worst robbers in the world. And this I say, that . . . And I don't care who you may be, but . . . but you, all of you, are full of hatred and envy towards me. You hate me of old, and this is your work, Botberg, this is your work ; you will take your revenge because you couldn't get me to lend you any money. But what sort of a fellow are you, I should like to know ! Or shall I tell you ? You are a drunkard, an adulterer . . ."

"Mr. Chairman, I beg to move . . ."

"Call *him* a chairman ! What right has he to be a chairman more than anybody else ? There he sits and turns over his papers, but deuce a bit does he know himself what they are all about. You are not a bit better than other people. Even your cows all die in the winter of dysentery, but my cows don't die. What do you make out of that dairy of yours over there, I should like to know ? How are you a bit better than other people ? You are neither more nor less than a paltry Government tenant, a peasant, a mere lodger, an ex-sergeant, a poor devil who . . ."

"My good friend, if you don't

hold your tongue and be off this instant, I'll tell the Board to catch you by the neck and chuck you out !" said the captain.[1]

"Talk Finnish if you can, and don't bully me! Let other people hear you ; let those peasant boobies outside hear what you have to say too ! Chuck me out ! Come along and try, that's all ! Ha, ha, ha ! I'd twist such a Board as this into a knot any day, and think nothing of it. Just move from the spot, that's all, and you shall go flying out of the window right under our horses, the whole lot of you ! What sort of people do you call yourselves, eh ? Will you say it yourselves, or shall I tell it you ? You are the biggest rascals, coxcombs, toadies in the whole parish, the whole lot of you ! You are poor rats, bone-pickers, meddlers with other people's pro-perty—swine ! You have never seen anything like real wealth, or even heard of it, or even had any wish to find out anything about it till you heard that I had something of the sort. And I *have* wealth, too ; I have more than you wot of. Seven thousand indeed ! That's

---

[1] This sentence is in Swedish.

a mere nothing ! I should be
ashamed to be taxed for so little,
if I put myself down at all. . . . I
should absolutely be ashamed. Put
down 10,000 while you are about it.
Or 100,000 or 200,000, if you like.
Write that in your book, Mr.
Chairman, if you can. Stick where
you are, and jot that down in your
book by the side of the 7,000. Here,
you may have my gloves into the
bargain, . . . take the gloves and
pawn 'em, if you like ! Hey ?"

"Constable, shut the door ! "

"Let the door be open, I say !
There should be no discussion here
with closed doors. I'll be off at
once, as soon as I've got my pelisse
on. But where's my quid of tobacco ? I musn't forget that.
Pfew ! There it is on the wall,
close to your ear, bailiff. Take it
off and stick it in your mouth.
Stick it in your mouth, I say, it is
nice and sweet ! And the members
of the Board may go home, and take
the shreds of their pipes along with
them. Yes, and you may add this
memorandum to your papers : tax
him on his two long pipe-stems,
that will make it all the more.
Hey ?"

"Chuck him out ! "

" Ha, ha, ha ! If I don't go of my own accord, you won't pitch me out. But I am going now. I've nothing more to say here for the present. I'll say more another time. Adieu ! "

Foaming with rage, he rushed out through the open doors, and flung the people assembled in the ante-chamber violently aside as he forced his way through them.

" My horse here ! " he yelled to his lad from the top of the steps with his hands to his hips. " Drive right up to the steps, will you ! A man who pays taxes on 7,000 is not going to drive from here like a mere pauper ! "

He threw himself at full length into the sledge, so that the seat cracked.

" Skip up behind, Pulkkinen, and off you go, Olli ! "

The horse reared and set off at full gallop.

" Your humble servant ! " he cried to the members of the Board, and plucking his cap from his head he swung it behind him in a half-circle again and again, now raising, now lowering it, so that sometimes it was high in the air and sometimes it was trailing along the road.

Only when the vestry-hall was
quite out of sight did he press his
cap deep down upon his head, and
adjust himself comfortably in the
sledge.

He was beaming with a bound-
less satisfaction, and when he wasn't
actually laughing aloud, his mouth
wore the whole time a broad grin.

" Ha, ha, ha ! I made their ears
tingle a bit. Hey ? Pulkkinen, you
heard how I gave it to them, didn't
you ? "

Pulkkinen was balancing himself
on the narrow rockers, first on one
and then on the other, and had considerable difficulty in sticking there
during the headlong flight.

. "What ? Did you hear ? Come
and sit here on the corner of the
sledge. You heard, I suppose, how
I gave it to them?"

"Yes, I heard it ; you laid it
across their backs a bit, certainly.
If I had been in the bailiff's place, I
should have been put to shame by
much less."

" Yes, indeed. Did you notice
how they looked ? What ?

" The bailiff pulled a very wry
face."

" You mean when I spat the plug
of tobacco right behind his ear ? "

" Yes, just then."

Hellman called that to mind, and
very much more that he had said.
And he laughed again and again,
and kept on putting fresh questions
to Pulkkinen.

" Hey, hey, hey!   They got it
hot for once !   Hey, hey, hey !   I
gave it them, didn't I ?   I let them
know what people thought of them,
eh ?   And they deserved it, too.
Did they pick up my quid from the
floor ?   Tell me, did they pick it
up ? "

" I didn't see them."

" They did, I know ; believe me
they did.   Hey, hey, hey !   But
tell me—did the bailiff stick my
quid into his mouth ?   I do believe
he's sucking away at it with all his
might at the present moment.   Hey,
hey, hey ! "

And all the way along he talked
of nothing but the same thing over
and over again.   And he seemed
never tired of laughing at it.

When he drove up to his house,
he did not go in at once, but stayed
outside while the horse was being
outspanned, and stroked and patted
it.

" Olli ! give the horse some oats ;
let it eat as much as it likes ! " he

bade the boy as he went away. Then he called to Pulkkinen, who was dragging the sledge into the shed.

"Come in and have a glass, Pulkkinen. We'll have a little schnaps on the strength of it. Come along!"

"I'll drag the sledge in first."

"There's no hurry about that; . . . let it be. . . . Olli can drag it in, for the matter of that."

Pulkkinen, however, dragged the sledge in all the same, and after that he strayed towards the stable.

"Can such a disturbance pass without an action at the assizes?" asked the ostler.

"No, certainly not; . . . the gentlemen would be out of their senses if they left it as it is . . ."

"One dog can't tread on another's tail and nothing come of it."

"Even if . . ."

"It will go ill with him, I suppose?"

"One hundred marks fine, I should say, perhaps 1,000, for insulting an official Board in open session, . . . or, if there's any luck in it, perhaps imprisonment into the bargain."

"Phew!" whistled the ostler.

III.

THE squire's good humour lasted so long that the rumour of it spread to all his neighbours, and one morning the wife of one of the cotters on his estate said to her old man—

" They say that the squire last week browbeat the magistrates and all the rest of them, and 'tis said that he's now in such a good humour as to be quite nice to speak to. Go, then, Antti, and have a talk with him, and get him to remit us this year's rent. You know we can't pay it with all that debt on our shoulders. Go and beg of him."

"What's the good? You saw how it fared with Aappo last autumn."

"Yes, it fared badly with him, certainly. Yes ; the rich gentleman is very hard when he sets his mind on a thing. But go and try, all the same."

" Very well ; I'll go."

Antti set out with a heavy step. On his way thither he stopped for a bit at a neighbouring farm, and sat down there on a bench, silent and depressed. The farmer's daughter-in-law was alone in the room, and was busy with her bread-shovel between the table and the oven.

"Any news from your way?" she asked.

"Nothing at all; and from yours?"

"No; nothing, . . . except that the squire seems to have left off raging; . . . at least, nothing has been heard of him in the village during the last few days."

"Indeed."

"Perhaps he has now begun to live like a human being."

"I don't know—I hope so."

The woman went out into the yard with the oven-mop, and when she came in again she said—

"He seems to be at the grain magazine; he must be selling rye, I should think."

Antti looked sorrowfully out of the window, and shortly afterwards quitted the room. He had to go across the fields to get to the squire's. There stood the squire in his short pelisse in front of the magazine, and seemed to be giving orders to some one in the upper storeys, the doors of which were open. The doors of the lower storeys were also open, and beyond the threshold was to be seen a fellow tying up the mouths of sacks with his hands and teeth. Another man was carrying them out to a sledge, which was drawn up close beside the steps of the magazine.

"Perhaps he'll be in a good humour now that he is selling grain," hoped Antti.

The squire now began to go towards the house, but, before following him, Antti strolled up to the magazine.

"Where are these sacks off to?" he asked.

"To the factory."

"How much a tun does he get for them?"

"The skinflint grabs like a swine. Thirty marks a tun he gets for it."

"D'ye mean to say he gets as much as that?"

"One is obliged to give it, because one cannot get grain elsewhere for love or money."

"Has he gone home now?"

"So they say."

Antti first cast a glance into the magazine, where the troughs were filled with grain right up to the ceiling. Then he went up to the hall. He carefully brushed away the snow from his boots before he went in.

"It will be no good coming here, I know," said he to himself, as he lifted the latch.

The squire had thrown his pelisse over a chair, and was sitting in his shirt-sleeves drinking coffee and eating wheat-bread. Pulkkinen was sitting on a chair by the door, and had just put some sugar in his coffee which the maid had presented to him.

"What business have *you* come about?" asked the squire; but he didn't bellow at him as usual.

Antti had not yet begun to bring forward his petition when an idea seemed to occur to the squire, and he said, while he was drinking his coffee—

"Harkye, Antti! ain't you going to pay your rent this year? It ought to have been paid last week, you know."

"That is just what I have come to talk to squire about."

"Have you come to pay?"

"I really couldn't pay just now. . . ."

The squire immediately began to get angry.

"Then what do you come running here for? Don't you know that if you have the use of my cottage and

land you ought to pay rent for it?
Hey?"

"It ought to be paid, I know, but
if a man can't?"

"Why can't you? You've had
a good year."

"It was not good. The frost
nipped the spring crops."

"Your own fault. You sowed
too late."

"I missed the seed-time because
I had to do manual service work
on squire's farm, and after that it
began to rain."

"I didn't make the rain. Am I
to suffer loss on your account?"

"If you will only wait a little for
your debt till I can manage to get
the next crop in, then I hope to be
able to pay off both debt and rent
at the same time."

"I can wait neither for my rent
nor for my debt. The debt has
already gone before the court, and
is in the bailiff's hands."

"But then my last cow must go."

"Let it go; I can't help its being
your last."

The squire stood smoking and
looking out of the window.

"There's another of those
beggars!" he cried. "They are
just such whiners as you. One

can make nothing of people here. The whole place is swarming every day with people like you ! "

" Hie ! you old hag ! " cried he, from the top of the steps (he had hastened there already); " turn back ! D'ye hear ? Don't try and get in here ! Go elsewhere ! No row here ! Be off ! Turn your wheel-barrow round and look sharp about it ! "

Antti cast a dull look towards the window and saw at the door a beggar-woman who was dragging a child after her on a wheelbarrow while an older child was shoving it on from behind. But when the squire again called to them, and in a still harder tone, stamping at the same time on the frozen, clatter-ing, hall floor, the old woman, who seemed to be utterly exhausted, turned her barrow round and began to toil away again along the snowed-up road.

" Yes," said the squire to Antti, when he had come in again, " I tell you it won't do. I can't wait for what is my due ; I'll wait for no-body, whoever it is. And why should I wait ? I can't let you have my property for nothing ! So bear in mind what will happen to you if the rye you have to bring me, by way of rent, is not within a week inside my barn."

" There does not seem to be room enough for the rye that's there already," said Antti half-aloud, with a bitter smile.

" What ? "

" Nothing, nothing ! " said Antti, and off he went.

" What did he say ? " the squire asked Pulkkinen, who had been sitting there and smoking all the time.

" I understood him to say that your barns are so full that they cannot hold what they have all ready."

" Oh ho ! So he's cheeky into the bargain, eh ! A set of scamps ! "

" Scamps indeed ! Why, even that Antti can't keep a cotter's holding going, though I always thought he could."

" Not one of them can—not a single one."

" If you would sell the holding to me I'd undertake to look after it and pay the rent in time."

" You ? What would you, a single chap, do with a cottage ? "

" I think it is about time I had

quarters of my own; I am quite
ashamed of living in lodgings. And
then, too, it has such a nice situation
on the shore of the lake."

"Would you really like to buy
the property?"

"I should like to buy the buildings, and you could have the use of
the fields and meadows. They are
in pretty good condition."

"Yes, he appears to have kept
them in pretty good order; but I
can't drive Antti out if he pays his
rent."

"He can't pay at all. If you
distrain for the amount of your
debt, what will he have to pay
with if you, immediately afterwards, sue him for the rent?"

Hellman made a hasty mental
calculation. "Twice two are four
—400—add another, that makes
500. H'm! Will you pay 200
for the buildings?"

"No doubt I might be able to
manage it."

"Then you may have it. But
Antti must be summoned pretty
soon, for the court will begin to sit
presently."

"When one talks of the devil!
—if there isn't one of the Board of
Assessors coming this way!"

"What the mischief does he want here?"

"Perhaps he's only out for a drive."

"Well, of course.   What else?"

But a suspicion had arisen within him and he began to walk uneasily up and down the floor, now and then pausing at the window to have a peep out.   The assessor did not seem to be in any particular hurry. He tied his horse to the gate-post, fished up a wisp of hay out of his sledge and threw it in front of his horse, spread the horse-cloth over its back, and then began to slowly make his way across the yard.   He was a big, stalwart sort of man, with a thin face and a calm look. Hellman tried to guess what his errand might be, but he could make nothing at all of it.

"Take a seat," Hellman forced himself to say when the assessor remained standing in the doorway without delivering his message.

"I have had quite enough sitting down already," said the member of the Board; but he sat him down all the same.

Hellman felt obliged to offer him tobacco also, though an evil foreboding began to gnaw away at his

5

breast more and more every moment. Pulkkinen saw very well what was going on within him. He knew the assessor's errand thoroughly, and he watched the behaviour of both with a crafty side-glance.

" It is very fine weather ; . . . not very mild perhaps, but not so freezing cold either," said the assessor, after lighting his pipe and leisurely beginning to smoke it. He drew short, graceful puffs, and looked steadily at the bowl of his pipe, wagging the tips of his toes all the time.

" It is nice winter weather, certainly," opined Pulkkinen.

"Does Mr. Assessor come from home ? " inquired the squire.

" Yes ; I was out of the house pretty early this morning."

" A good many summonses, I suppose ? " said Pulkkinen.

" Yes, there are one or two of that sort, too."

The maid-servant brought in two cups of coffee—one for Pulkkinen, the other for the squire.

"Give it to the assessor ! "

While he was drinking, the squire couldn't help asking if he had any business with him.

" Oh yes, I've business with you, Squire, too."

"Go away Pulkkinen, and then the assessor can . . . "

"No need for him to go away, . . . indeed it is a business that must be done in the presence of witnesses."

Hellman was quite certain now that it was a summons.

"Do you wish to serve me with a summons, then?" stammered he.

The assessor sipped up the last drop of his coffee from the saucer, replaced his cup upon it, and transferred his teaspoon from his knee to his saucer. Then he put the whole lot on the table, took up his pipe from the floor, where it had stood leaning against the table, and carefully lit it. It was only after taking several whiffs that he said—

"Serve a summons? Yes."

"And wherefore? Hey? At whose instance? Is it for debt? Do I owe anybody anything?"

"It is not for debt at all."

The assessor stood up, placed the pipe in its proper place on the shelf, and said, with a hard, official voice—

"It is not for debt, but for defamation of character which took place last Tuesday in the vestry-hall. You are summoned to appear before the court on Monday next,

by Captain Steelhammer, on behalf
of the Board of Assessors."

"Oh, indeed, indeed! Ha, ha,
ha! Indeed! H'm!"

Squire Hellman had become
quite confused. At the very first
sight of the assessor he had begun
to fear as much, but he would not
listen to his own foreboding. And
now it came upon him like a thunder-
bolt from a cloudless sky. And the
confident and dignified bearing of
the assessor prevented him from
bursting forth into invectives.

"For defamation of character?
Oh, indeed! And when did *I* ever
insult him, I should like to know?"

"As my instructions are to
summon you before the court, you
must know all about it."

"And do you fancy I shall appear
there at any summons of his? You
may quite make up your mind that
I shall do nothing of the sort."

"As to that you may please yourself . . ."

"Who told you to summon me?"

"The captain gave me the money
for the purpose."

"Tell him I don't mean to come;
. . . so he needn't fancy I shall.
You may strike the summons out of
the judge's list. . . . It is quite an

unnecessary trouble—an altogether
unnecessary trouble."

"It is time that I went now,"
said the assessor, as he shook hands
at parting.

When the assessor had shut-to
the door, Hellman made as if he
would have followed him. But he
thought better of it and turned
instead to Pulkkinen.

"Harkye, Pulkkinen! do you
think anything will come of it?"

"I don't know the law. It
might."

"Go and ask the assessor what
he thinks. Go at once, before he
has ridden off. He is untying his
horse already. But don't ask him
as if I had sent you. Pretend to
ask as if it was on your own
account."

While Pulkkinen was talking to
the assessor, who was standing and
holding his horse-cloth, which he
had taken from the horse to put
back into the sledge, Hellman per-
ceived the empty coffee-cups on the
table. Furious at the sight, he
rushed through the saloon to the
dining-room door and bellowed
from thence to the maids in the
kitchen—

"Why don't you take those cups

away? What the deuce is the meaning of such sluttishness? Are they going to remain there all day? Why don't you answer, you hussey! Hey?"

"Mercy upon us! I didn't come before because . . . "

"What! and you dare to bandy words with me! If you dare to open your mouth, I'll discharge you on the spot! Quick march, I say!"

He stood in the doorway, and, with outstretched hand, beckoned to her to pass by. With a sobbing in her throat the girl hastened towards the cups, and Hellman followed close upon her heels. The whole time the girl had a terrified feeling that the moment she got to the table and began taking up the cups he would seize her by the hair and tear it out by handfuls.

But the same moment Pulkkinen came in and the girl succeeded in getting away.

"Well, what did he say?"

"He said that it is a 100 marks' fine business, and that you'll be very lucky if you don't get locked up as well."

"Eh? No; it can't be. No; lies! He knows nothing. . . . He

lies. . . . He only wants to frighten
me."

" An assessor ought to know, I
should think."

" He knows about it no better
than other people. It can only be
50 marks at the very utmost.
Imprisonment, indeed ! I don't
believe it. I don't believe a bit of
it."

But he *did* believe it, and his eyes
began to gleam more and more with
fear.

Pulkkinen pretended to be going.

" Harkye, Pulkkinen, don't go
yet. . . . How much did he say the
fine would be ? "

" He said that it was 100 marks
to insult the court in session, but
that it might mount to many thousands. And it is said that very often
money alone will not settle it."

Hellman's hair was altogether in
disorder, and there was a twitching
about his mouth just as if he were
on the point of weeping.

" A hundred—1,000 marks' fine !
—1,000 marks' fine and perhaps
imprisonment into the bargain. . . .
But perhaps they only want to scare
me with their summonses. Do you
believe they are really in earnest
about it ? What ?"

" That's just what I asked the assessor myself, and he said that they certainly were in earnest."

" What ! They really are in earnest ! Yes, of course they are. . . . Of course they won't let it pass. A pack of wolves ; . . . regular scamps, the whole lot of them."

" The assessor thought that perhaps they might be inclined to look the matter over if something were paid them . . . "

" If something were paid ? "

" But they certainly wouldn't otherwise."

" Not otherwise ! . . . Of course. . . . Otherwise, indeed ! They won't be content with a mere trifle ; I know them ; . . . they'll keep a firm grip when once they've got hold of one ; . . . regular wolves, that's what they are."

" But a little hard cash would help you through, anyhow."

" I'd rather be locked up ! "

" Nobody can tell beforehand, you know, how the court may look upon the matter."

" I know very well how it will be. . . . They have no mercy whatever ; . . . they all have an old grudge against me ; . . . they are just like so many lawyers. Oh, oh ! " he groaned, " what a calamity, what a calamity ! "

Tearing his hair and moaning aloud, Hellman went right through all the rooms of the house one after another. More than once Pulkkinen made as if he were going, but Hellman wouldn't let him go.

" What are you in such a deuce of a hurry for ? . . . You have nothing to call you away so soon. Wait a bit. Don't go ! Can't you sit down, man ? "

" Wouldn't it be best to try and come to terms with them ? "

" It certainly would be best, it certainly would be best ! Go, Pulkkinen, and tell them to inspan. Tell them to inspan at once. Woe is me, what a calamity ! "

All the people in the house were amazed to see the squire looking out from the yard-door so silent and subdued, and most of all the serving-maid. No bellowing and bullying, no abuse and blackguarding, as it always had been heretofore. The squire tottered about just like an old man, and when he sat in the sledge he groaned like a sick man.

" Give the reins here ! " said he to the lad in a pitiable, almost humble tone, and guided the horse

himself in a dull, dead-alive sort of
way.

"He is like a whipped cur[1]
now!" said the lad to Pulkkinen,
as he watched the departure of his
master.

But the squire drove on and on,
and thought himself the unluckiest
man in the whole world. He was
hated and persecuted. They had
all conspired against him. If one
brought an action against him all
the others would follow suit. One
can always find a reason for doing
so if one only takes the trouble to
look for it. The best fellow in the
world is bound to have a rough time
of it, if one betakes oneself to in-
trigues and advocates.

He was driving now upon the ice
where a sharp blast blew the ice-
mingled sleet right into his face and
ears. The blast was blowing sideways, and chilled first his right shoulder and his whole right side, penetrated through to his left shoulder,
and gradually chilled his whole body.

The sleet wet the collar of his
pelisse, and the moisture dripped

---

[1] *Uittetu Koira; lit.*, "A dog that has just
come out of the water dripping wet."

down from thence upon his neck
and into his bosom. He trembled
and shivered as if he would have
shaken his limbs asunder.

His evil conscience took advantage of the defenceless wretch's depressed state of mind, and began to
knock and tap in every direction as
if it would have risen up bodily
from the bottom of the sledge.
Gradually it succeeded in making
yawning chasms in one or two un-
sound spots in his life, and from
these chasms there grinned at him
many a deed which had long since
sunk into the background of his
thoughts, or had even slipped out
of his memory altogether. Amongst
other things he now saw the shining
silver rubles and the crisp bank-
notes, one or two of which had,
from time to time, slipped into his
pocket when he stood behind the
counter of the Councillor of Commerce at Uleaborg. The Councillor
of Commerce was a rich man, and
it didn't matter very much to him,
thought Hellman. But the Avenger hasn't made any inquiries about
it yet, it occurred to him. Perhaps
it was only now that he was about
to begin his work of destruction.
What if he had only let him keep it

for a while in order to demand his
own again all the more peremp-
torily? Perhaps now he meant to
turn everything topsy-turvy? And
now, behind the silver rubles and
the crisp bank-notes, popped up
smaller trickeries in the horse trade;
his own hard words to the helpless
and needy sounded in his ears with
a dull roar and a dark swarm of
indistinct, rag-wrapped shapes,
amongst whom appeared the beggar-woman with her child and her
barrow whom he had lately driven
away, rose up before him. All this
drove him quite into an agony, and
he tried violently to close these
chasms of conscience, but the more
he tried the more widely they
yawned apart. Then he tried not
to mind it and to shut his eyes to
it. He told himself that it was
only some one who wanted to
frighten him, and he was deter-
mined to show that some one that
it was of no use trying.

But it was of no use at all to keep
a stiff upper lip, and the rotten
places would *not* close. Then
cowardice got the upper-hand of
him and made his soul tremble in
the same proportion as the cold became more sensible and the frozen

sleet smote against his face. And
the persuasion that the Avenger
had now begun to attack him, and
had set all this on foot, got, every
moment, a harder grip upon his
soul. It was the Avenger and
nothing else that had blinded him
and led him to insult them all in
the vestry-hall so as thereby to
give his enemies power over him.
The Avenger was cunning and
skilful, and could trip up and fling
over just when one was least on
one's guard.

And now his soul began to fumble
instinctively after some weapon
wherewith to drive away the Avenger and defend himself against its
assaults. He sought for long and
found nothing, but at last he hunted
out of the nooks and crannies of
his memory a good deed which
might serve him as a weapon. And
now that he *had* got it in his hands
he held it steadily before him and
flourished it about like a scarecrow.
It was an old beggar-woman whom
he had once taken up into his sledge
as he was going the self-same way,
and thus saved from being frozen
to death. The old woman had
dragged herself along the snowed-
up way with her child, and would

very soon have been frozen to death
there upon the ice if he hadn't
helped her, made her sit in the
sledge, and covered her with the
furs.   Nay, he had actually sat him
down on the coachman's box, although it was intensely cold and
blowing hard.   In this way he had
driven home, and there the woman
had got something to eat and had
been taken care of for nearly a fort-
night.   And the child had even had
sweet biscuits given to it, and the
woman herself coffee.   And they
weren't even poor people from his
own parish, but she had come from
somewhere or other a long way off
by the Gulf of Bothnia, and she
had a few odds and ends of news to
tell about the squire's own birthplace.   She had also been a good
laundress, and had worked for the
squire and all the manor-house
folks.   But a good deed is a good
deed for all that, and he could have
found no end of washerwomen
among his own tenants.

As he bethought him of this he
began to regain his confidence, and
the yawning chasms beneath him
seemed to grow smaller.   And now
he had got over all the ice.   The
horse that hitherto had been pain-

fully struggling onwards through the snowdrifts, suddenly dragged the sledge at a gallop up the high bank, the bell on the thill tinkled merrily, and the depressing thoughts vanished.

"Hey!" cried he, and smacked with the reins to put some go into it. What rubbish it was to sit there and worry about his sins! Was he any worse than others?

And when Squire Hellman approached the captain's house and drove rattling into the courtyard, all the so lately yawning chasms had closed up, so that it was just as if his conscience were beneath a carefully-laid-down pavement. No gaps were visible anywhere, and no seams either. It was a perfectly hard, smooth surface.

IV.

THE bailiff had come on a visit to the captain a little before Hellman drove into the yard.

"If there isn't the wolf! . . . look, there he is!" cried the pair of them, when they saw Hellman drive into the courtyard.

"He has come to make it up;

what else should he have come for?
. . . We'll pretend that we have
just been laying our heads together
about it ; we'll have a fine joke out
of this."

It must have been a really capital
joke, for they both laughed heartily.

"It will be so comical to see . . ."

"Pst ! He's in the lobby already.
Keep your countenance, mind ! . . .
I'll stand here and listen all the
time. . . ."

The bailiff had just managed to
slink into the room alongside when
Hellman stepped in.

He came in pretty pluckily, and
pitched his cap and gloves upon a
chair.

"Good-day !" said he, as uncon-
cernedly as usual.

The captain had sat down hastily
at the table, put on his glasses, and
was pretending to read something.
He let it be seen that he had heard
some one come in, but it was only
after some time that he raised his
head and regarded his visitor over
his spectacles.

"Good-day !" he replied, coldly
and slowly, affecting at the same
time to be unpleasantly surprised,
and without stirring from the spot.

Hellman had intended to behave

as if bygones were bygones, but this reception deprived him of the self-assurance that was already beginning to come back to him on the road. Nevertheless he attempted to keep it up, and came forward to shake hands. Although the pressure of the captain's hand was tepid, still it encouraged Hellman to take a seat upon the sofa uninvited. Meanwhile his eyes began to wander shyly round the room, and all about the roof and walls, for the captain said nothing. There he (the captain) continued to sit with his head turned on one side to conceal his merriment, which he had some difficulty in repressing.

" Is there anything in which I can be of service to you, brother ? " he inquired at last, very solemnly.

"Why, yes! There's that awkward affair of mine. . . . Think nothing of it. Let it pass! We'll say no more about it. . . . Why should we fellow-parishioners bring suits against each other for such trifles? "

And he tried to smile and waved the whole affair contemptuously away from him with one hand.

"It is well, my friend, that you admit it to be an awkward affair.

6

Awkward it really is, . . . especially
for us."

"Well, well! don't bother about
it any more! What's the good?
Let's make it up!"

"Ah! So you're inclined to
compromise it, eh? H'm! So,
brother, you would make it up?
H'm! Of course, of course! I'm
glad to hear you say so."

"Just so. What shall we gain
by going to law about it? After
all, it is a mere bagatelle. And
what's the use of a lawsuit, except
to set silly tongues a - wagging?
Let it rest where it is. I suppose
we may take that as settled?"

The captain continued sitting
there with averted head, but he
squinted from time to time at the
crevice of the door where one of
the bailiff's eyes was twinkling.

"H'm!" and again he coughed
resolutely. "Are you aware,
brother, of the legal penalty for
such conduct?"

"No, I am not; . . . but in any
case, I suppose, it is not much, . . .
a mere bagatelle."

"It all depends by what name you
choose to call it. Perhaps you will
permit me to show you the article
of the code which deals with this

sort of thing. . . . Be so good as to come and read for yourself."

The captain had the code ready opened at the corresponding place, and he laid it on the corner of the table. Hellman came forward and stood by the table, but bade the captain read.

" Because I haven't got my glasses with me," he said, by way of excuse.

" ' Imperial statute on false accusation, *and other defamation of character*, dated November 26, 1866,' " read the captain, following the text with his finger.

" ' Paragraph 7 : Every one who of set purpose disparages another in his quality of citizen, or attempts to *shake confidence in him in his official or magisterial capacity* . . .' that's just what you've done."

" Well, well, but how does it go on after that ? "

" ' . . . Either by word, sign, or written representations, which he circulates himself or causes to be circulated, or falsely accuses him of any definite offence, or of such actions as may bring him into public contempt, shall be punished for such libel by hard labour for a period ranging from two months to two years, or with imprisonment from one month to one year, or with fines from 500 to 1,000 marks."

"Ah, indeed! H'm! Very good! But is this law in force now?"

"It has just been sanctioned. Look for yourself."

"Yes, yes; . . . it seems all right; . . . I see, I see."

"It is a strict paragraph."

"But isn't the lowest fine there 50 marks?"

"Yes, but it can't apply to the case in point. To insult a court in open session comes under the head of offences punishable by the severest penalties . . . "

"I don't believe it."

"Then if you don't believe it, the court must decide."

"There were extenuating circumstances. . . . I was not exactly sober."

"You were perfectly sober. Every one could see that before you began your blackguarding."

"I was not sober, I say; . . . I was out part of the time, remember."

"That is really very remarkable, for I have been told that you did nothing all the time you were out but flog your innocent horse."

Hellman could answer nothing to this, so he was silent and bit the end of his moustache.

" Well, well ! let us compromise the matter, then. Why can't we compromise it ? "

" Willingly, so far as I am concerned. . . . The matter doesn't bother me very much. . . . I am quite agreeable to settling things amicably, . . . but I don't know how the . . . "

A gleam of comfort ran through Hellman's body. He took the captain's hand.

" Thanks, brother ! thanks, brother ! " [1] said he.

" There's nothing to thank me for. *So far as I am concerned*, it is all right, but I don't know how it is with the others. The bailiff's case is the worst. You insulted him more than anybody else."

Hellman had fancied himself out of the scrape, and now he found himself worse in it than ever.

" It would therefore be best," continued the captain, " for you to go and talk it over with him at

---

[1] This is in Swedish. He uses the *official* language of the country to curry favour with a Government official.

once, and try to get him to agree to a compromise."

"I'll go. I'll go this very instant. ... Perhaps he *will* agree to it. ... What do you think? Don't you think he'll agree to a settlement?"

"Possibly."

"Has he said anything?"

"I haven't met him lately."

"But what did he say when you saw him? Was he angry?"

"Well, I must say he *was* pretty angry then."

"Angry no doubt he was. ... He is spiteful, and treasures up his grudges. But don't you think he might consent to a compromise? Don't you think he would?"

"One cannot tell."

"Perhaps I had better go to him now. What do you think?"

"I don't quite know what's the best thing to be done."

"I'll go on the spot. It's all in my way home. I shall be passing close by. Brother, you are a splendid fellow. I know nobody like you, indeed I don't. Adieu! Look in at my place now and again, dear friend. You show yourself so very seldom though we are neighbours. And now, good-bye!"

"Why in such a hurry? Sit down and have a smoke."

"Nay, nay! I should like a smoke very much, . . . many, many thanks. . . . But not this time. . . . I must hasten to the bailiff . . . "

"You needn't be in such a mortal hurry."

"But he might be leaving the parish, you know, . . . so I really must. . . . Pray excuse me."

"Very well, then. Adieu!"

"Adieu, brother. Greet your wife from me, and don't forget to look in. . . ."

Out he went, urgent and obsequious, and the same instant the bailiff came out of his hiding-place. The captain and he saw through the window how Hellman unfastened his horse from the paling and hastened out into the driving snow. They laughed heartily at the practical joke they had played him, and at last the captain said—

"But aint we a little too hard upon the fellow?"

"Hard be hanged! The Shylock! Let him feel for once what it is to be dependent on others."

"It would be great fun to see what he does when he doesn't find you at home."

" When he hears that I am here,
he will turn his horse's head and
come hither again."

" He'll scarcely come here again,
I think."

" You'll see that he will. I'll
stake my head upon our having him
again this afternoon."

The candles had scarce been
lighted when, sure enough, Squire
Hellman came driving into the
captain's courtyard for the second
time, just at duskfall.

The captain and the bailiff were
sitting with their toddy - glasses
beside them when a tramping and
a fumbling after locks was heard in
the lobby. At last a man encased
in snow to his very eyebrows entered
the room. In the course of the day
the wind had gone round to the east,
and brought with it a regular snow-
storm.

They had told Hellman at the
bailiff's that he had gone to see the
captain quite early that very day.
Hellman had immediately turned
round and driven the shortest way
back. He hadn't even given himself time to look in at home, and
all through the long journey his
one thought had been, " Now they

are laying their heads together, I
must hasten thither as fast as I can,
or the bailiff will make a fool of the
captain, and win him over to his
side."

Towards the end of the journey,
however, a suspicion arose in his
mind—

"How comes it that I haven't
met the bailiff on the road ? "

And on the heels of this suspicion
followed another—

" Perhaps the sneak of a fellow
was with the captain while I was
there.   And no doubt it was his
sledge that I saw a little outside
there."

A couple of versts from the house
he passed one of the captain's men
with a waggon-load of hay.

"Is the bailiff at your place ? "
he asked.

"I don't know if he is still there ;
but he was certainly there this
morning . . . ."

But instead of being furious at
being made a fool of, he only became
still more meek and humble.

" Good   afternoon,"   said   he,
timidly, as he came in.

"Good afternoon, good afternoon,"
replied the others, amicably. " Pray
take a seat, brother."

With a suspicious glance at the
pair of them, and combing his wet
beard with his fingers, Hellman sat
down on a chair close to the sofa.
His host offered him tobacco and
toddy, but he took neither. Then
the captain and his guest went on
to talk of good weather and bad, of
snowstorms, and cold blasts, and
tried to drag Hellman also into the
conversation. He was compelled to
take part in it now and again, so as
to have an opportunity of introduc-
ing his own errand. At last the
captain went out to fetch some hot
water for more toddy, and then
Hellman turned to the bailiff.

"I have been to seek you about
this business of ours ; . . . the captain
has told you about it, of course ? "

"No! What business is it ? "

"It is that . . . that . . . affair . . . in
the vestry-hall . . . you know what
I mean. . . . Don't you recollect ? "

The bailiff was puffing away at
his pipe all the time.

"Oh, *that*—oh—ay ! . . . Well,
what about it ? "

"Well, I've been summoned about
it, . . . but we needn't let it go
before the court, need we ? "

"Why not ? We shall get at the
bottom of it better that way."

"Nay, don't let us do that ; . . .
let's come to an arrangement about
it like honourable men."

The bailiff puffed away and said
nothing, so that Hellman was compelled to add—

"And, besides, I'll pay something
by way of compromise if . . . "

"H'm ! That's all very well ; . . .
but you abused me, recollect, in the
coarsest manner ; you called me a
rogue, a drunkard, and adulterer."

"I didn't say adulterer."

The bailiff took offence at once.

"You didn't say it ? You mean
to say you didn't ? I tell you you
said all that and much more too. . . .
You insulted me to my face—me, a
servant of the Crown, at a public
session of the Board."

"All I did was to let my quid of
tobacco fall on the floor."

"Let it fall, did you say ? I tell
you you jerked it out of your mouth
with your middle finger and aimed
it straight at me ; it was no thanks
to you that it did not hit me, for you
meant it to. Let me tell you that
I won't stand such things, that I
won't put up with a public insult
offered to those whose office and
duty it is to maintain order and
watch over public security. Do you

know what the penalty is for such
conduct ? "

" Yes, I do ; . . . it is very serious,
I know ; . . . but my temper got the
better of me, . . . and I don't know
what I do when I get into a temper."

" That's nothing to do with me.
The law must decide."

The bailiff had got angry in real
earnest as he recalled the circum-
stance, and he paced angrily up and
down the floor with his hands behind
his back. Hellman followed hard
after him, and offered objections and
excuses all the time.

" Nay, but listen, my dear friend :
don't let it go before the court ; . . .
take back the summons, dearest
friend ! . . . I'll pay any composition
you like ; . . . take it back, dear
friend ! . . . The captain promised to
accept a compromise ; . . . now,
didn't you, Captain ? "

" Yes, I did promise," said the
captain, as he placed the hot-water
can on the table.

" Then why can't you also ? . . .
Come, overlook it now, dear friend !
. . . Don't bring me into trouble ; . . .
I'll pay whatever you like."

" You'll pay as much as I like,
will you ? "

" Yes, yes ; anything in reason."

"Oh! I know very well what you mean by 'anything in reason.' ... I know you; you won t pay a single penny unless it goes into court."

"I'll pay, I tell you; . . . I'll pay on the spot. How much will you have?"

"But money payment is by no means the main thing," said the captain. "The main thing is to apologise."

"That I have done already, and I now do so again."

"Yes, to us perhaps. But what's the good of that, even if you went on begging our pardon all your life, when you have to make it up with the whole Board?"

"The whole Board?"

"Yes, precisely. Your abusive language was directed at the whole lot of us, and every one of them has given me a power of attorney."

"Oh, alas, alas! Oh, woe is me, woe is me! Now I am lost indeed—lost and ruined for ever and ever! ... Woe, woe is me!"

When the bailiff had enjoyed his grief and lamentation for a time, he said—

"Well, suppose now my stupid good-heartedness were to try and help you? But, recollect, I do it out

of pure goodness of heart. You
really don't deserve it."

" Oh, help me, dear friend. Don't
be hard upon me."

" Have *you* never been hard on
anybody ? "

" I have not been very . . . "

" Don't you rack and flay your
own tenants, for instance ? "

" Hark ye, Botberg," interrupted
the captain, " what business is it
of yours how he treats his tenants ?
. . . that's *their* look out."

" I suppose it is. . . . But, as I
said, I can try what I can do with
my colleagues, though I really don't
know what will come of it. But, if
by any means I can, I'll try and
help you out of the fix."

" Ah, try it, dear friend—do try !
Talk to the others, and try to bring
them round. Don't some of them
owe you something ? "

" There can be no question of
force here."

" No, no, of course not. No
question of force, but . . . "

" The only thing that I can think
will be of any use is a public
apology."

" Yes, yes . . . "

" At least I shall insist upon it, so
far as I am concerned, and the

captain, I think, will insist upon it likewise."

"Certainly," said the captain, with his nose in his glass as he took a swig at the toddy.

"And the others will insist upon it too, remember."

"Yes, yes."

"In short, you must publicly, in the presence of strangers, beg pardon of us all whom you have so grossly insulted."

"Yes, yes, I'll do that right enough. . . . When shall I do it?"

"You had better leave the whole matter absolutely to me, otherwise . . ."

"Absolutely to you, then, . . . naturally . . ."

"In the ordinary course the matter would come before the court on Monday. . . . The afternoon before, you may come to the saloon of the court outhouse, and thither I'll bring, as witnesses, all those whom it concerns."

"You'll bring witnesses?"

"All for your own good. Besides, it isn't legal otherwise."

"But, anyhow, don't bring many: . . . two or three, perhaps?"

"That's my business."

"Of course, of course."

"And instead of your paying a composition to each one separately I'll try to get them to agree to pass the evening pleasantly together at the expense of him whom it most nearly concerns . . . "

"Yes, and in what way?"

"Well, I'll get some one to lay us a bit of supper with suitable dishes, and liquor beside, according to our requirements."

"Yes, yes."

"Do you agree to this?"

"Yes, . . . of course. . . . It won't be . . . it can't be a . . . I have never made similar arrangements myself, but it won't be a regular banquet, I suppose?"

"A banquet? That depends upon what you call a banquet. Well, let it be a banquet then, if you like. Have you anything else to say?"

"Nothing, nothing! One cannot tell beforehand, I suppose, how much it will cost?"

"I don't know, I'm sure; . . . but if you are going to cavil about a few dozen marks or so, why, let it go before the court—it's all the same to us."

"No, no; I didn't mean that. . . . I merely meant to say . . . it will

be jolly like that, of course—oh, yes.
. . . H'm."

So the matter was settled, and
after a short pause they began to
talk of something else. But, somehow, so far as Hellman was concerned, the conversation would not
flow easily. He was very thought-
ful and absent, and let his pipe,
which the captain had insisted upon
lighting for him, gradually go out.
When he had sat there a little time,
he got up, took his leave, and went
out.

But in the lobby he turned round
again, and, standing in the doorway,
begged the bailiff to come out for he
had something to say to him.

"I want . . . I mean to say
I should like . . . this . . . this
banquet not to cost too much
money. . . . I am a little hard-
pressed for money just now . . .
and so one might perhaps tell the
hostess at the inn to send and buy
their meat, fish, and milk from us,
and you might also get your cook
from us, and also the dishes for the
feast all ready cooked ; . . . although,
I suppose, it will not be a regular
banquet after all ; . . . yes, yes."

"Harkye, brother," said the
bailiff, "either we'll leave the whole

7

thing to the hostess, or if you won't
hear of that, why, then let us simply
go before the court, and then you
will be quit of the whole thing."

"No, no, by no means ; . . . not
at all. . . . Adieu ! "

"But the story must be well
circulated, eh ? " laughed the bailiff,
as he reported this last conversation
to the captain.

"It certainly will be the drollest
thing out," opined the captain ; "at
the same time, however," added
he, "I'm a bit sorry for the fellow
too."

"Deuce take the skinflint ! " said
the bailiff.

"By all means, if you like,"
admitted the captain, and there-
upon they rubbed their hands and
laughed heartily at their quaint
conceit whereby they had succeeded
in making the greatest screw in the
whole parish stand them a banquet.

"We'll invite as many strangers
as the house can hold," said the
bailiff ten times at least in the
course of the afternoon.

"Didn't you notice how humble
he was the whole evening ? So it
always is when a man has no back-
bone, let him be never so rich.
Why, a thing like this warms a

man's body down even to his little
toe."

" A toast on the strength of it."

And they toasted each other.

But Squire Hellman drove home
through the night with very varying
feelings. The road was snowed up
again and progress was slow and
painful. At first he urged on the
horse by shouting, and when that
wouldn't do he grew angry and
seized the whip. The horse sprang
forward for a few paces but very
soon stumbled along again, foot by
foot, in the deep drifts. So at last
Hellman had to resign himself to
it.

There were two thoughts and two
circumstances which plagued him
alternately. First, there was the
gnawing sensation that he had been
made fun of, and perhaps always
would be. And then he fell to
brooding over the possible cost of
this banquet. It was certainly
bound to cost as much as the others
liked. It was they and they alone
who had to arrange all about the
meat and drink and invite the
guests. He tried to tot up how
many they would probably invite,
but he dared not make an estimate
of all the items which might be

considered necessary. Suddenly the
banquets of the Uleaborg Councillor of Commerce occurred to him.
At these there had always been
champagne and dessert as regular
things ! But surely it could never
come to that here ! They could
never be so downright godless as
that, eh ? But who could answer
for them ? They were capable of
anything, . . . and they had an old
grudge against him. . . .

Towards the end of the journey
he was almost lamenting aloud.
And when he got home, at last, he
was positively ill. He puffed and
blowed, and spoke with a whine in
his voice, and deep wrinkles lay
across his forehead. His wife had to
help him off with his pelisse and
the other wraps, and drag off his
overshoes.

" What's the matter ? Are you
sick ? " his wife attempted to say.
But he gave no answer.

" Have you a headache ? Or have
you caught a chill, perhaps ? Shall
I make you a little tea ? "

" No, leave it alone ! "

" Perhaps a little rubbing would
do you good ; . . . it is your old
neck-complaint, I am sure. . . . Let
me try . . . "

"What the mischief are you
bothering about ? . . . Leave me
alone, can't you, . . . and be off
about your business, you old cat,
you !"

He gave his wife a vicious blow
with one hand, so that she fell into
a chair ; she gave a short shriek
and began to cry for fright and
blubber in her apron.

"Blubber away, that's right ! . . .
You're all alike, both at home and
abroad."

In his fury he again threw his
pelisse over his shoulders, rushed
headlong out, banged the door
behind him with all his might, and
went to his own room. Then he
quickly locked the door, wrapped
himself in his pelisse, and cast
himself on the sofa to sleep as best
he could.

V.

THERE was a general rejoicing
among the gentry of the parish
when it became known that Hellman had been compelled to give a
banquet to which the bailiff was to
invite the guests. They had all
some sort of grudge against Squire
Hellman, if for no other reason,

because he was rich ; and now, whenever two people met together, they enjoyed this good bit of news to the full. In every homestead to which the bailiff conveyed the news, everybody rubbed his hands with joy ; and both when he arrived and when he departed, the bailiff always said in precisely the same way, " Ha, ha ! the story fills me with delight, even down to my little toe ! "

" Serve him right ! So, for once, he also has fallen into the trap, the old fox ! " the others always added.

The bailiff had invited all his acquaintances as " witnesses," and the other parties to the suit had done the same thing. So that just at the time when the court was beginning to sit, all the advocates, solicitors, record-clerks, officers of the court, assessors, bridge-inspectors, and all other persons in any way connected with the court, licked their chaps and made ready to pass a very pleasant evening at Squire Hellman's expense. Besides these, the judge, the doctor, the apothecary, and half-a-dozen shopkeepers were also invited to do honour to the occasion.

The little church-town was also a

market-town, and there was a capital
inn there. The large room of this
inn, which was also used as a court-
house, was hired for the evening's
entertainment. The court-table and
the judge's bench were both removed
and put up against the wall. The
Bible and the code-book were hoisted
up on to the highest shelf of the
dusty book-case. In their stead the
largest bread-table of the bakehouse
had been set up in the middle of the
floor, covered with a white table-
cloth, and there the loving-cup was
to be drunk as an introduction to
the evening's banquet. Round
about the walls were placed smaller
tables, on which toddy-boards,
bundles of cigarettes and ash-trays
had their proper places. Everything
was arranged on the most genteel
scale, and the bailiff had not limited
the entertainment to a "little re-
freshment," but had ordered a regular
sit-down *supé*.[1]

The landlady, assisted by a
waiting-maid, placed glasses alongside the bowls all down the table,
on both sides ; and the landlord,
who was also a storekeeper, had

---

[1] *Illallinen*, the usual word, is an ordinary
supper ; *supé* a supper on a grand scale.—*Tr.*

brought in cigarettes from his store
for the smaller tables, and poured
cognac out of a flask into the
decanters.

" Will you have the lobster up
from the cellar for supper ? " asked
the landlord.

" Yes, certainly ; . . . it'll only
spoil if you don't. . . . Hellman
shall put some money into our
pockets for once in a way."

" He can well afford it. . . . He
generally has all he wants from
Uleaborg, even down to salt, . . .
but this time a little crumb or two
of the profit he makes will fall into
our pockets."

" Besides, this Hellman fellow is
a regular sharper."

" Let him pay, then ! How many
bundles of cigarettes shall I lay on
each table : . . . two, eh ? "

" Put three, or four," said the
landlady ; " the more you put down,
the more will be taken up ; . . .
when there are plenty and to spare,
you'll see how the people will keep
on taking up fresh ones and throw
away the old ones when they are
only half smoked."

" Well, now, haven't I said over
and over again that you are much
more sensible than I? . . . It is not

every one who has such a sensible old woman as I have," said the landlord.

The fat landlady nudged the serving-maid, gave her a look, and whispered—

"He talks as if it were he who had all the goods. Fie upon him!"

And indeed the landlady did own the shop, and everything else, and it was she who ruled the roast. She had made her bookkeeper her second husband, and ruled and reigned herself without intermission.

Towards seven o'clock the guests began driving in to the courtyard. The bailiff arrived first—as became a host—and received the others. He ordered, straight off, that a lamp should be put in the lobby, and that plenty of candles should be put upon the table and in the window-sills, so that the guests might not have to grope their way in, and that all the world outside might know that there was just as big a banquet going on as if it were a wedding. It was quite unnecessary to spare any expense. It was no pauper who would have to pay for it.

"Be so good as to come right in,

gentlemen ; . . . a little further ! . . .
that's right. . . . And now a little
cognac all round ; . . . the very
best thing in the world when one
comes out of the cold ! . . . Kippis !
fetch some sugar and cold water !
Here's lots of tobacco, cigars, and
cigarettes, let everybody take whatever he likes best ! . . . Come now,
set to ! " cried the bailiff, heartily ;
and, as the guests arrived, he con-
ducted them to the upper part of
the room.

The doctor came, carrying his big
paunch along with him. The judge
came, and trumpeted with his big
nose. Even the apothecary came
creeping in, very much exercised as
to where he should bestow his hat,
and when he had found a place for
it at last, behind the flower-pots in
the window, he grasped his long
beard and carefully combed it out
with a comb which he took out of
his pocket ; . . . only after that did he
light a cigarette and join the others.
Then the captain arrived in his
big wolf-skin pelisse, and when he
got out of it, he came into the room
in a neat, snug morning-coat, carefully shaved, his moustaches beauti-
fully trimmed, and his own pipe in
his hand. After that came all the

other members of the Board, the
recorders, advocates, the judge's
assistants, and several of the richest
farmers of the parish.

The bailiff invited the new
arrivals to sit down and smoke.

" Sit down and smoke, and make
yourselves quite at home," he said
incessantly ; and added in a whisper
to each one of them, with a knowing
smile : " *The guest of the evening*
has not yet arrived, . . . but that
makes no difference, . . . we can
begin without him."

" *The guest of the evening !* " they
all cried, and burst out laughing.
First they laughed with the bailiff,
and then they laughed among themselves, bent regularly double, and
then straightened themselves out
again, and hitched their waist-
bands.

The captain followed the example
of his leader, and stuck his head
into every group which had formed,
to laugh over the "guest of the
evening."

" A deuce of a joke, . . . ain't
it ? "

" Spendid material for a comedy,"
said the doctor, who was a bit of a
dramatist himself at home ; "it would
have an astonishing effect if only

there was some one who could com-
pose it."

"Yes, by George! how magnifi-
cent it would be. Altogether extra-
ordinary. But how did you get him
to agree to it ? "

"He couldn't help himself—
couldn't help himself, I tell you.
. . . It was really my invention,
he, he, he ! When I was a lieu-
tenant and saw something of the
world, we had a similar affair with a
comrade who had been just as
stupid "—and now he told the whole
tale from beginning to end—"now
isn't that the very best way to
punish such a fellow, eh ? "

"It is indeed, no doubt about
it ; . . . and others can get some fun
and pleasure out of it, too."

"Did you hear how we let him
drive backwards and forwards ? "

"In sleet and snow, yes, indeed !
. . . The bailiff has told us about it
already. . . . But one can scarcely
believe that Hellman would let
himself be fooled like this . . ."

"He was obliged to—obliged, I
say; he, he, he! He was so scared
when *imprisonment* stood before him
and threatened him! He, he,
he !"

"What the deuce ! Imprison-

ment for a trumpery affair like
that ? "

" Wist, wist ! That's the law.
But we won't say anything more
about that till to-morrow ; . . . hold
your tongue this evening, . . . he,
he, he ! "

They all laughed, for in everybody's opinion the thing was now as
droll again, and the practical joke
of the bailiff and the captain was
now the subject of conversation in
every group.

But the bailiff began to think that
Hellman was loitering a little too
long, so he went out into the kitchen
and gave orders that toddy-water
was to be brought in.

" As the guest of the evening
doesn't seem to have arrived yet,
and we hold the office of hosts, . . .
why, let us begin," and he began to
put lumps of sugar in the glasses.
But now the boots came in and said
that Squire Hellman begged him to
come out. He wanted to speak to
him a moment.

" Why doesn't he come in ? "

" He is sitting there in his sledge,
and sent for you."

" What the deuce is it ? " grumbled the bailiff, but out he went.
One or two scriveners immediately

skipped after him to peep through
the door-cracks.

"Is he still sitting in his sledge?"
asked the rest.

"He is getting up now."

"Why doesn't he come in?"

"He won't come in this way. He
is saying that he would rather come
through the back shop.... Keep still,
a fellow can hear nothing if you
keep on talking. 'Are there many
strangers?' he is asking. The
bailiff is telling him: not many. ...
'Whose are all these horses?' asks
he.—'Oh! so he noticed them!'—
Ts! The bailiff says, 'What are you
bothering your head about the
horses for?' Deuce take it, here he
comes!"

They hastily drew back, for the
same instant the bailiff opened the
door and shoved Hellman in by the
shoulders. All the guests stood up,
and those who were moving about
stopped and bowed to the fresh
arrival. He replied to their greetings
first of all with an embarrassed
cough, but afterwards with a couple
of awkward bows.

The bailiff urged him to take off
his pelisse, and one of the scriveners
came to take it. Then the captain
came up and shook hands with him,

and he and the bailiff led him further into the room, past the bowing group at the table. Hellman could only blurt out such fractional greetings as : " Good-day ! H'm ! Good afternoon !—You here ?—Yes. —No!" and when he had got past the lot of them, he invited the bailiff to come with him into one of the side rooms.

" Shall I apologise straight off ? "

" Yes, as soon as the punch-bowl is ready."

" What! a punch-bowl, too ? "

" Naturally ! How else would you have it ? "

" Of course, of course ! "

" You go in, and I'll go and make them hurry up with the punch-bowl."

" Listen ! Don't go yet ! I . . . I think I should like you to do it instead of me ! "

" You mean apologise ? "

" Yes, it will be all the same if you . . . I mean to say I am no great hand at . . ."

" Why not ? Of course I can do it if you are present in the room at the same time ; . . . and now just go in and fill a pipe for yourself and brew your own toddy. . . ."

"I can very well wait here till . . ."

"Just as you like, . . . but when you hear me tap the corner of the bowl, mind you come in."

"All right, all right."

The bailiff left Hellman in the back shop and went himself into the saloon and thence into the next room where the landlord and the captain were brewing the punch-bowl. Thither assembled gradually around them groups of inquisitive assessors and a number of farmers who had never seen this marvel before.

"That's something like a brew, that is," said one of them.

"Wouldn't it be just as good to eat the sugar by itself and drink the cognac and the wines just as they are?"

"No, it is better this way."

"There, stop! That's quite enough cognac. Now add a couple of bottles of wine!" ordered the apothecary.

"Take four and another bottle of cognac besides," urged the bailiff.

"It will be too strong!"

"And too dear!"

"That's nothing to do with it. I mean it to be good, cost what it will.

You don't want to drink sugar-water here, I suppose ? "

"How dear is it as it stands, I wonder ? "

"Taste it, and don't ask questions."

"Let me taste it too! . . . by George, though, it *is* good ! "

"Nothing like what it will be, though. Fetch hither a couple of bottles of champagne ! "

"No ! Deuce take it, no ! "

"What are you chattering about ? I tell you champagne is always put in the best punch-bowls."

And they all laughed knowingly, and looked at each other.

The bowl was mingled, and all sorts of good things were chucked into it till, at last, the bailiff and the apothecary both agreed that it would do, although it could still perhaps bear another bottle of wine or two.

" 'Tis good ! " and after that the bowl was borne in and everybody followed after it.

All this time Hellman was sitting in the back shop and heard, through the walls, the measured clinking of the silver ladle against the sides of the bowl and at the same time, through the other wall, from the kitchen, the clattering of dishes and

the savour of a jolly good roast
penetrated to him.   An incalculable
quantity of oaths and wicked words
were tumbling about inside him, but
they didn't pop out.

He writhed about on a chair, got
up and walked a few steps, stopped,
listened, and sat down again.

At last he heard from the saloon
a furious tinkling, and he went in.

The bailiff was already standing
up, glass in hand, and the innkeeper
was filling the last glasses at the end
of the table out of a milk-can.   All
the others had also stood up and
turned their looks towards Hellman,
who was standing by the door.

The bailiff tinkled once more
with the ladle at the side of the
punch-bowl and began his speech.

"Gentlemen !   H'm !   Well, I
think I may say that we all know
what has brought us together here
to-day, . . . so that I need not
waste any more words about that.
Shame upon all grudge-bearing, say
I !   What do you say ? "

" Yes, yes," resounded from every
quarter.

"It was all owing to a mistake,
and show me the man who doesn't
forget himself sometimes.   To err is
human.   But on behalf of him

whom it immediately concerns, I
merely beg that you will forget all
old grudges and be friends, and that
the whole thing may be allowed to
drop.   What do you say ? "

"Yes, yes, Hellman is a fine
fellow ! "

"Then let us drink his health !
Long live Hellman ! "

"Hurrah, hurrah ! "

That was the whole speech, and
while they hurrahed they clinked
glasses.   Those who hadn't succeeded in getting glasses procured
coffee-cups from the kitchen and
filled them out of the punch-bowl.
The bailiff gave a glass to Hellman,
clinked glasses with him and gave
him his hand, and so did all the
others, both the principals and
the witnesses ; first the judge, then
the doctor, then the apothecary,
and so on in graduated order of
rank.   When this had been done,
the bailiff and the captain came up,
took Hellman by the hands and led
him to the seat of honour on the
sofa.   On the table, in front of the
sofa, was placed a milk-can full of
punch, and around it assembled a
circle of gentlemen and a few assessors, while the others made themselves uproariously merry at the

other end of the room and drank and smoked incessantly.

But Hellman all the time could not rightly appreciate the honour paid to him. The bailiff had stuffed a cigar into his mouth almost by force, and Hellman sucked clumsily away at it, and sat there very ill at ease with his stiffly starched collar cutting his neck, and razor scars on his recently shaved face. His hand trembled a little as he held the cigar or lighted it, for it went out in the meantime.

"Here's a light!" said the bailiff. "Don't bother yourself any more about this little affair, Hellman; . . . we were all of us a little bit out of temper, I suppose, and shame upon him who bears a grudge, say I. . . . We won't say anything more about it. Your health!"

"Your health, brother!" said the captain also, who was sitting there in a very happy frame of mind with his eyes blinking a little, his own pipe between his teeth and his toddy-glass in front of him, for he was independent of the punch-bowl. "If I can catch you any time at home, I thought of coming to have a peep at that young horse of yours; . . . they say it's splendid."

" It is a handsome horse enough."

" You have the best horses in the whole parish."

"In this way," began the bailiff again, " we shall best get this awkward affair cleared up, in this way we shall get out of it most comfortably, and nobody can say a word ; for my part, I have not the least grudge left . . . "

"Nor we either . . . "

"And if any one says that Hellman is not a fine fellow, he'll have to let *me* know the reason why. Harkye, how about your execution against Antti, . . . are you in any hurry about it ? "

" Well, I should like to hasten on with it . . . "

"Good. I'll have the auction advertised in church to-morrow morning for next week so that you may have your money in hand at once. They are such rogues, these cotters."

" Rogues they are indeed," interrupted a farmer, eagerly, " there's no doing anything with them, . . . they won't pay their debts from year's end to year's end, and they don't do their service at the set times, they don't look after their fields, and they never clear their land properly either."

"But perhaps the reason is that the farmers put too heavy burdens upon them?"

"That's a barefaced lie; shut your mouth! You don't know anything about it."

"Come, come, we won't quarrel about that!" said the captain. "Your healths!"

"Your health, Hellman! Don't be in a bad humour! Drink, man, that you may feel to-morrow morning that you really have been at a banquet. . . . Bring some more punch here!"

"'Tis all gone!"

"All gone already?"

"Good wares don't wait for customers."

"Hie, toddy there! of course we didn't mean that one bowl to last the whole evening. . . . Brew some more toddy, my good friends!"

Hellman sat there like a stranger in his own house, like one whose goods are being sold under his very nose by other people. He heard everything that was spoken in the room, followed every single person with his eyes, and calculated the cost of every glass that was drunk and every cigarette that was smoked.

He sweated inwardly for sheer

vexation when he saw how only half-smoked cigarettes were pitched upon the floor and fresh cigarettes were constantly being lighted. And the storekeeper was never weary of bringing in fresh supplies from his store. Ten marks' worth of them had already been consumed, to say nothing of the cigars, . . . and they all seemed to have a wager who could drink the most. Glass after glass was emptied, and again and again the bailiff lifted the empty decanters and loudly ordered them to be refilled.

He was pretty drunk already, and so were many of the others.

"Come, don't stand upon ceremony ; drink away, my friends. Hellman has left the whole management of the thing to me, so that when I say drink, drink you must. Drink yourself, too, Hellman ! . . . don't look so down in the mouth, man ! Drink ! . . . you are let off jolly easily, you know. . . . Your health ! "

"Then the bailiff twisted his head first to the right and then to the left, and burst into a violent peal of laughter.

"Deuce take it, what a raging lion you were ! Hey, hey, hey ! One

can scarcely recognise you sitting
there so meekly and looking so
mump - chance. . . . You black-
guarded us like I don't know what;
. . . deuce take it ! Do you recollect
how you spat your plug of tobacco
right into my face ?   Luckily it
didn't hit the mark, but struck the
wall.   It was a lucky thing for you,
and you may thank your stars that
it did not hit me.   Your health,
man ! . . .   Why, your glass is
empty !   Give it here, I'll brew you
a regular stiff jorum !"

"I don't want any ; . . . I must
go home."

"Won't you stay to supper ? "

"What ! will there be a supper as
well ? "

"Naturally.   Don't you see they
are laying the table-cloth ? "

"Of course I see that.   But are
they *all* going to eat ? "

"Certainly, and at your expense,
as we arranged."

"All the people here ? "

"Certainly.   Didn't we say so ?
You had better stay.   It will be a
capital supper.   Come, stay ! "

"No, I can't ; . . . I don't feel
very well."

"Well, I can't help it, then. . . .
Harkye, good friends ! "

" Stop !   What are you going to do ? "

" Only tell them you want to say good-bye ! "

" No.   Say nothing ! "

" I tell you I will.   Listen, good friends and honoured guests ! "

But the uproar was already so great and the room so full of tobacco-smoke that they could neither hear nor see one another. Besides, the bailiff's voice was now quite hoarse so that only those nearest to him could hear him.

" Don't make a row ; . . . I'll steal away quietly ; . . . what's the good of making a to-do about it ? "

The bailiff followed him to the door, and there he stood, with legs apart, and watched Hellman putting on his pelisse beside the stove. And all the while Hellman saw them laying the table inside and bringing up bottles of beer and flasks of wine and placing them all down the table with little intervals between each. He could count a dozen bottles of beer already, and half a dozen flasks of wine.   And more and more came up every moment from the back shop.

" No more, my dear friend, no more ! . . ."

"What do you mean?"

"Don't let them fetch any more wine and beer. . . . There they come again, with as many as they can hold . . ."

"You set your mind quite at ease and hasten home and go comfortably to bed, and don't grumble. But recollect also that if the account is not paid to-morrow, it is not a very long way from here to the court-house. And now good-bye, and be off!"

Even this Squire Hellman was obliged to swallow down. He crept out through the door and sat down in his sledge which had been waiting for him all the time before the steps. As he drove past the window he heard shouting and loud laughter and saw people moving about behind the hazy window-panes.

"It will be *my* turn one of these days," the boy heard him hiss. The boy dared not turn his head, but he fancied, as he glanced sideways, that his master took a good long look behind him and clenched his fist while he hissed—

"Wait a bit, you scoundrels, that's all! It will be my turn one of these days!"

*   *   *   *   *

At an unlucky hour on the following day Antti came again to
beg for a respite for the payment of
his debt.   Perhaps he would be
luckier on a Sunday, his wife had
said.

" I won't go any more—no good
will come of it," protested Antti ;
but he went all the same.

At the very moment when Antti
entered, Squire Hellman had before
him an account for 200 marks,
and the innkeeper was waiting
at the door.   Antti would have
drawn back if he could, but as it
seemed to him no go, he remained
standing by the door and stared
dreamily before him.   Pulkkinen
was also there, and sat in his usual
place in front of the pipe-shelf,
smoking away with an innocent expression of face but furtively obser-
ving the others.

" This is too much ; I won't pay
it, I tell you. . . . There, take your
account back.   I'll only pay half ;
the rest you may pay yourself."

At first he had said he wouldn't
pay a penny, then he had offered to
give a fourth of it, and now he went
up to a half.

" The whole of it must be paid,
. . . so the bailiff said."

" What ! The whole of it ? 200 marks ? Never in this world. I'll pay for the liquor, but the others may pay for what they ate. . . . I ate nothing, . . . and, as I said before, I'll pay half. . . . There's 100 ; take it ! Hey ? "

" The whole of it must be paid ; . . . I won't take a single penny if you don't pay the full 200."

" Then let it alone. So much the better for me. My money will go back into the bank, that's all. They'll take care of it for me there, I warrant."

" And then they told me to greet you, Squire, besides, and say that if the account was not paid, a fresh summons will arrive before midday, . . . although there's no need of that, for the former summons has not yet been withdrawn."

" You are a pack of the greatest rascals, villains, rogues . . ."

" It's of no use blackguarding ; lay down 200 marks on the table, and I'll go. . . . You had best not irritate me any more, but leave well alone, or else you'll get into a fresh scrape ; . . . in any case you'll be compelled to pay the account."

" I'll not be compelled. If I pay it at all, it will be of my own free will.

I am not such a poor devil as those
gentlemen in town. They can't
even pay for what they eat. Look,
now! . . . there you are! Take it ;
. . . no, I won't ; . . . you sha'n't
have new ones, . . . a dirty bank-
note is good enough for you."

" It's all the same to me."

" And now pack yourself off at
once, and don't come here again."

" I'll go willingly enough, without
being asked."

And the innkeeper went, but he
had scarcely reached the lobby when
Hellman rushed after him.

" Those rascals can never close the
door behind them ! "

Then was heard a pair of bangs
which made all the windows rattle :
it was Hellman shutting the lobby
door. When he came back again
he fell foul of Antti.

" What are *you* doing here again ? "
he bellowed.

" I come about the old business
which . . ."

" Pack yourself off. . . . It's no
good. I'm in want of money. You
saw just now how I as good as
chucked 200 marks into the sea."

" Is it I, then, who am to pay for
your banquets ? "

" Hey ? "

"I only mean to say—am I to be robbed of all I have simply that you may be made a fool of by the gentry?"

"You hold your jaw; and if you don't take yourself off headlong and go your road . . ."

"Ah, yes! the road indeed lies open before me now; . . . to the beggar the road has no end, he has plenty of elbow-room there, God knows. . . . Adieu!"

"A pack of rogues! There they stand with the beggar's staff already in their hands, and they presume to be insolent into the bargain!"

"Yes, that's how they are, . . . the poorer the bolder," said Pulkkinen; "I suppose I may have the property now?"

"Wait a bit! Did you hear if they remained there long last night?"

"At dawn of day the last of them departed. The bailiff was carried to his sledge unconscious." .

"Regular swine, I call them; and they are the lords and masters of the parish! Fie upon them!"

"I can't quite understand how you, Squire, could be got to pay for their feast."

"I couldn't help myself. If it had

come before the court I should have
been sent to gaol."

"Go along ! I thought so myself
at first, but the judge is said to have
declared that at the very utmost it
would perhaps have been a fine of
200 marks."

"Don't lie ! . . . It would have
been imprisonment, I tell you. . . .
I know very well that . . ."

"So he is said to have declared,
anyhow ; . . . of course I don't know
the ins and outs of it, but so he said,
they say."

"But I have read the paragraph
myself, and I know very well . . ."

Hellman already began to doubt
himself, but he couldn't yet believe
that things were so.

"I saw the paragraph, I tell you,"
insisted he ; "I saw it with my own
eyes ! . . . Well, to change the subject, do you want to buy this property?"

"Yes, I should like to, if we can
agree about the price."

"What will you pay ?"

"Two hundred. So you see you'll
get back the very sum you have
just lost."

"What's that got to do with you?"

"And in this way the banquet
will have cost you nothing."

" How so ? "

" Why, hasn't Antti raised all those buildings, and now you'll get 200 marks for them."

" But the timber is from my woods."

" What's the timber worth, I should like to know ? "

" H'm, h'm ! If it is as you say," and Squire Hellman's face brightened more and more. He hadn't thought of the matter in that light before. Things fitted in splendidly. Actually, the very sum !

" But have you the money to pay it with ? I won't let a single penny remain on credit."

" A dealer in timber is never without money. You shall have the money down on the nail, and brand-new, clean notes they shall be into the bargain."

Pulkkinen fished up his note-book from his breast-pocket, unloosed its many bands, and picked out from it eight brand-new 25 mark notes and totted them up on the corner of the table.

Hellman rattled the keys of his safe in his trousers' pocket, and could not refrain from smiling a little. He took the money, held them up to the light to see if they were genuine, and opened his till. Then he cautiously laid his money in the empty space which had lately arisen there. When this was done he carefully closed the drawer, raised the flap and turned the key.

And he felt as if the cog-wheels of his world had gripped each other fast again, after being for several days deranged.

And life at the squire's house rolled along, for a long time, as lightly and softly as when one drives on a recently oiled car. Pulkkinen was a daily guest there, and there they sat so cosily and talked again and again, with a sly laugh, of the wonderful luck of fortune's golden laddy Hellman, who never could be driven into a corner so it seemed : what he lost out of one hand came immediately back into the other.

And the gentry of the parish still laugh and roar over their own great craftiness at having compelled Squire Hellman to give a banquet to which *they* invited the guests.

But Antti goes begging his way along with his wife and child, wandering wearily onwards and regarding with dim, dull eyes the course of this world where the poor man has so little to expect . . . and so very seldom gets even that little !

WHEN FATHER BROUGHT HOME THE LAMP.

WHEN father bought the lamp, or a little before that, he said to mother :—

" Harkye, mother — oughn't we to buy us a lamp ? "

" A lamp ? What sort of a lamp ? "

" What ! Don't you know that the storekeeper who lives in the market-town has brought from St. Petersburg lamps that actually burn better than ten *päreä* ?[1] They've already got a lamp of the sort at the parsonage."

" Oh yes ! Isn't it one of those things which shines in the middle of

---

[1] A *päre* (pr., *payray* ; Swed., *perta* ; Ger., *pergel*) is a resinous pine chip, or splinter, used instead of torch or candle to light the poorer houses in Finland.

the room so that we can see to read in every corner, just as if it was broad daylight ? "

" That's just it. There's oil that burns in it, and you only have to light it of an evening and it burns on without going out till the next morning."

" But how can the wet oil burn ? "

" You might just as well ask— how can brandy burn ? "

" But it might set the whole place on fire. When brandy begins to burn you can't put it out even with water."

" How can the place be set on fire when the oil is shut up in a glass and the fire as well ? "

" In a glass ? How can fire burn in a glass—won't it burst ? "

" Won't what burst ? "

" The glass."

" Burst !   No, it never bursts. It might burst, I grant you, if you screwed the fire up too high, but you're not obliged to do that."

" Screw up the fire ? Nay, dear, you're joking—how *can* you screw up fire ? "

" Listen, now ! When you turn the screw to the right, the wick mounts—the lamp, you know, has a wick, like any common candle—and

a flame too, but if you turn the
screw to the left, the flame gets
smaller, and then, when you blow it,
it goes out."

"It goes out! Of course! But
I don't understand it a bit yet, however much you may explain—some
sort of new-fangled gentlefolk arrangement, I suppose."

"You'll understand it right enough
when I've bought one."

"How much does it cost?"

"Seven and a half marks, and the
oil separate at one mark the can."

"Seven and a half marks and the
oil as well! Why, for that you
might buy *päreä* for many a long
day—that is, of course, if you were
inclined to waste money on such
things at all, but when Pekka splits
them not a penny is lost."

"And you'll lose nothing by the
lamp, either! *Päre* wood costs
money too, and you can't find it
everywhere on our land now as you
used to. You have to get leave to look
for such wood, and drag it hither to
the bog from the most out-of-the-
way places—and it's soon used up,
too."

Mother knew well enough that
päre wood is not so quickly used up
as all that, as nothing had been said

about it up to now, and that it was
only an excuse to go away and buy
this lamp.   But she wisely held her
tongue so as not to vex father, for then
the lamp and all would have been
unbought and unseen. Or else some
one else might manage to get a lamp
first for his farm, and then the whole
parish would begin talking about
the farm that had been the *first*,
after the parsonage, to use a lighted
lamp. So mother thought the matter
over, and then she said to father :

" Buy it, if you like, it is all the
same to me if it is a *päre* that burns,
or any other sort of oil, if only I can
see to spin. When, pray, do you
think of buying it ? "

"I thought of setting off to-morrow
—I have some other little business
with the storekeeper as well."

It was now the middle of the
week, and mother knew very well
that the other business could very
well wait till Saturday, but she
didn't say anything now either, but
" the sooner the better," thought
she.

And that same evening father
brought in from the storehouse the
big travelling chest in which grand-
father, in his time, had stowed his
provisions when he came from Ulea-

borg, and bade mother fill it with
hay and lay a little cotton-wool in
the middle of it. We children
asked why they put nothing in the
box but hay and a little wool in the
middle, but she bade us hold our
tongues, the whole lot of us. Father
was in a better humour, and ex-
plained that he was going to bring a
lamp from the storekeeper, and that
it was of glass, and might be broken
to bits if he stumbled or if the sledge
bumped too much.

That evening we children lay
awake a long time and thought of
the new lamp ; but old scullery-
Pekka, the man who used to split up
all the *päreä*, began to snore as soon
as ever the evening *päre* was put out.
And he didn't once ask what sort
of a thing the lamp was, although
we talked about it ever so much.

The journey took father all day,
and a very long time it seemed to us
all. We didn't even relish our food
that day, although we had milk-
soup for dinner. But scullery-
Pekka gobbled and guzzled as much
as all of us put together, and spent
the day in splitting *päreä* till he had
filled the outhouse full. Mother,
too, didn't spin much flax that day
either, for she kept on going to the

window and peeping out, over the ice after father. She said to Pekka, now and then, that perhaps we shouldn't want all those *päreä* any more, but Pekka couldn't have laid it very much to heart, for he didn't so much as ask the reason why.

It was not till supper-time that we heard the horses' bells in the courtyard.

With the bread crumbs in our mouths, we children rushed out, but father drove us in again and bade scullery-Pekka come and help with the chest. Pekka, who had already been dozing away on the bench by the stove, was so awkward as to knock the chest against the threshold as he was helping father to carry it into the room, and he would most certainly have got a sound drubbing for it from father if only he had been younger, but he was an old fellow now, and father had never in his life struck a man older than himself.

Nevertheless Pekka would have heard a thing or two from father if the lamp *had* gone to pieces, but fortunately no damage had been done.

" Get up on the stove, you lout ! " roared father at Pekka, and up on the stove Pekka crept.

But father had already taken the lamp out of the chest, and now let it hang down from one hand.

"Look! there it is now! How do you think it looks? You pour the oil into this glass, and that stump of riband inside is the wick —hold that *päre* a little further off, will you!"

"Shall we light it?" said mother, as she drew back.

"Are you mad? How can it be lighted when there's no oil in it?"

"Well, but can't you pour some in, then?"

"Pour in oil? A likely tale! Yes, that's just the way when people don't understand these things; but the storekeeper warned me again and again never to pour the oil in by firelight, as it might catch fire and burn the whole house down."

"Then when will you pour the oil into it?"

"In the daytime—daytime, d'ye hear? Can't you wait till day? It isn't such a great marvel as all that."

"Have you *seen* it burn, then?"

"Of course I have. What a question? I've seen it burn many

a time, both at the parsonage and when we tried this one here at the storekeeper's."

" And it burned, did it ? "

" Burned ?   Of course it did, and when we put up the shutters of the shop, you could have seen a needle on the floor. Look here, now! Here's a sort of capsule, and when the fire is burning in this fixed glass here, the light cannot creep up to the top, where it isn't wanted either, but spreads out downwards, so that you could find a needle on the floor."

Now we should have all very much liked to try if we could find a needle on the floor, but father hung up the lamp to the roof and began to eat his supper.

" This evening we must be content, once more, with a *päre*," said father, as he ate ; " but to-morrow the lamp shall burn in this very house."

" Look, father !   Pekka has been splitting *päreä* all day, and filled the outhouse with them."

" That's all right.   We've fuel now, at any rate, to last us all the winter, for we sha'n't want them for anything else."

" But how about the bath-room and the stable ? " said mother.

" In the bath-room we'll burn the lamp," said father.

That night I slept still less than the night before, and when I woke in the morning I could almost have wept, if I hadn't been ashamed, when I called to mind that the lamp was not to be lit till the evening. I had dreamt that father had poured oil into the lamp at night and that it had burned the whole day long.

Immediately when it began to dawn, father dug up out of that great travelling chest of his a big bottle, and poured something out of it into a smaller bottle. We should have very much liked to ask what was in this bottle, but we dursn't, for father looked so solemn about it that it quite frightened us.

But when he drew the lamp a little lower down from the ceiling and began to bustle about it and unscrew it, mother could contain herself no longer, and asked him what he was doing.

" I am pouring oil into the lamp."

" Well, but you're taking it to pieces! How will you ever get everything you have unscrewed into its proper place again ? "

Neither mother nor we knew

what to call the thing which father took out from the glass-holder.

Father said nothing, but he bade us keep further off.   Then he filled the glass-holder nearly full from the smaller bottle, and we now guessed that there was oil in the larger bottle also.

" Well, won't you light it now ? " asked mother again, when all the unscrewed things had been put back into their places and father hoisted the lamp up to the ceiling again.

" What ! in the daytime ? "

" Yes—surely we might try it to see how it will burn."

" It'll burn right enough.   Just wait till the evening, and don't bother."

After dinner, scullery - Pekka brought in a large frozen block of wood to split up into *päreä*, and cast it from his shoulders on to the floor with a thud which shook the whole room and set in motion the oil in the lamp.

"Steady ! " cries father ; " what are you making that row for ? "

" I brought in this *päre*-block to melt it a bit—nothing else will do it—it is regularly frozen."

" You may save yourself the

trouble, then," said father, and he winked at us.

" Well, but you can't get a blaze out of it at all otherwise."

"You may save yourself the trouble, I say."

" Are no more *päreä* to be split up, then ? "

" Well, suppose I *did* say that no more *päreä* were to be split up ? "

" Oh ! 'tis all the same to me if master can get on without 'em."

" Don't you see, Pekka, what is hanging down from the rafters there ? " When father put this question he looked proudly up at the lamp and then he looked pity-ingly down upon Pekka. Pekka put his clod in the corner and then, but not till then, looked up at the lamp.

" It's a lamp," says father, " and when it burns you don't want any more *päre* light."

"Oh !" said Pekka, and, without a single word more, he went off to his chopping-block behind the stable, and all day long, just as on other days, he chopped a branch of his own height into little faggots ; but all the rest of us were scarce able to get on with anything. Mother made believe to spin, but her supply of flax had not diminished by one-half when she shoved aside the spindle and went out. Father chipped away at first, at the handle of his axe, but the work must have been a little against the grain for he left it half done. After mother went away, father went out also, but whether he went to town or not I don't know. At any rate he forbade us to go out too, and promised us a whipping if we so much as touched the lamp with the tips of our fingers. Why, we should as soon have thought of fingering the priest's gold-embroidered chasuble. We were only afraid that the cord which held up all this splendour might break and we should get the blame of it.

But time hung heavily in the sitting-room, and as we couldn't hit upon anything else, we resolved to go in a body to the sleighing-hill.

The town had a right-of-way to the river for fetching water therefrom, and this road ended at the foot of a good hill down which the sleigh could run, and then up the other side along the ice rift.

"Here come the Lamphill children," cried the children of the town as soon as they saw us.

We understood well enough what they meant, but for all that we did not ask what Lamphill children they alluded to, for our farm was of course never called Lamphill.

"Ah, ah! We know! You've gone and bought one of them lamps for your place. We know all about it!"

"But how come you to know about it already?"

"Your mother mentioned it to my mother when she went through our place. She said that your father had bought from the store-man one of that sort of lamps that burn so brightly, that one can find a needle on the floor—so at least said the justice's maid."

"It is just like the lamp in the parsonage drawing - room, your father told us just now, I heard him say so with my own ears," said the innkeeper's lad.

"Then you really have got a lamp like that, eh?" inquired all the children of the town.

"Yes, we have; but it is nothing to look at it in the daytime, but in the evening we'll all go there together."

And we went on sleighing down hill and up hill till dusk, and every

time we drew our sleighs up to the
hill-top, we talked about the lamp
with the children of the town.

In this way the time passed
quicker than we thought, and when
we had sped down the hill for the
last time, the whole lot of us sprang
off homewards.

Pekka was standing at the chopping-block and didn't even turn his
head, although we all called to him
with one voice to come and see how
the lamp was lit.   We children
plunged headlong into the room in
a body.

But at the door we stood stock
still. The lamp was already burning
there beneath the rafters so brightly
that we couldn't look at it without
blinking.

" Shut the door ; it's rare cold,"
cried father, from behind the table.

" They scurry about like fowls
in windy weather," grumbled
mother from her place by the fire-
side.

" No wonder the children are
dazed by it, when I, old woman as
I am, cannot help looking up at it,"
said the innkeeper's old mother.

"Our maid also will never get
over it," said the magistrate's step-
daughter.

It was only when our eyes had got a little used to the light that we saw that the room was half full of neighbours.

"Come nearer, children, that you may see it properly," said father, in a much milder voice than just before.

"Knock the snow off your feet, and come hither to the stove, it looks quite splendid from here," said mother, in her turn.

Skipping and jumping, we went towards mother, and sat us all down in a row on the bench beside her. It was only when we were under *her* wing that we dared to examine the lamp more critically. We had never once thought that it would burn as it was burning now, but when we came to sift the matter out we arrived at the conclusion that, after all, it was burning just as it ought to burn. And when we had peeped at it a good bit longer, it seemed to us as if we had fancied all along that it would be exactly as it was.

But what we could not make out at all was how the fire was put into that sort of glass. We asked mother, but she said we should see how it was done afterwards.

The townsfolk vied with each other in praising the lamp, and one said one thing, and another said another. The innkeeper's old mother maintained that it shone just as calmly and brightly as the stars of heaven. The magistrate, who had bad eyes, thought it excellent because it didn't smoke and you could burn it right in the middle of the hall without blackening the walls in the least, to which father replied that it was, in fact, meant for the hall, but did capitally for the dwelling room as well, and one had no need now to dash hither and thither with *päreä*, for all could now see by a single light, let them be never so many.

When mother observed that the lesser chandelier in church scarcely gave a better light, father bade me take my A B C book, and go to the door to see if I could read it there. I went and began to read— "Our Father." But then they all said, "The lad knows that by heart." Mother then stuck a hymn book in my hand, and I set off with:—"By the waters of Babylon."

"Yes ; it is perfectly marvellous!" was the testimony of the townsfolk.

Then said father, "Now if any
one had a needle, you might throw
it on the floor and you would see
that it would be found at once."

The magistrate's step-daughter
had a needle in her bosom, but
when she threw it on the floor it
fell into a crack, and we couldn't
find it at all—it was so small.

It was only after the townsfolk
had gone that Pekka came in.

He blinked a bit at first at the
unusual lamplight, but then calmly
proceeded to take off his jacket and
rag boots.

"What's that twinkling in the
roof there enough to put your eyes
out?" he asked at last, when he had
hung his stockings up on the
rafters.

"Come now, guess what it is,"
said father, and he winked at
mother and us.

"I can't guess," said Pekka,
and he came nearer to the lamp.

"Perhaps it's the church chandelier, eh?" said father, jokingly.

"Perhaps," admitted Pekka; but
he had become really curious,
and passed his thumb along the
lamp.

"There's no need to finger it,"

says father ; "look at it, but don't
touch it."

"All right, all right! I don't
want to meddle with it!" said
Pekka, a little put out, and he
drew back to the bench alongside
the wall by the door.

Mother must have thought that
it was a sin to treat poor Pekka so,
for she began to explain to him that
it was not a church chandelier at
all, but what people called a lamp,
and that it was lit with oil, and that
was why people didn't want *pareä*
any more.

But Pekka was so little enligh-
tened by the whole explanation
that he immediately began to split
up the *pare*-wood log which he had
dragged into the room the day
before. Then father said to him
that he had already told him there
was no need to split *pareä* any
more.

"Oh! I quite forgot," said
Pekka ; "but there it may bide if it
isn't wanted any more," and with
that Pekka drove his *pare* knife
into a rift in the wall.

"There let it rest at leisure," said
father, but Pekka said never a word
more.

A little while after that he began

to patch up his boots, stretched on
tiptoe to reach down a *päre* from
the rafters, lit it, stuck it in a slit
faggot, and sat him down on his
little stool by the stove. We children saw this before father who
stood with his back to Pekka,
planing away at his axe shaft under
the lamp. We said nothing, however, but laughed and whispered
among ourselves, " If only father
sees that, what will he say, I
wonder ? " And when father did
catch sight of him, he planted
himself arms akimbo in front of
Pekka, and asked him, quite spite-
fully, what sort of fine work he had
there since he must needs have a
separate light all to himself ?

"I am only patching up my
shoes," said Pekka to father.

"Oh, indeed ! Patching your
shoes, eh ? Then if you can't see
to do that by the same light that
does for me, you may take yourself
off with your *päre* into the bath-
house or behind it, if you like."

And Pekka went.

He stuck his boots under his arm,
took his stool in one hand and his
päre in the other, and off he went.
He crept softly through the door
into the hall, and out of the hall

into the yard. The *päre* light flamed outside in the blast, and played a little while, glaring red, over outhouses, stalls, and stables. We children saw the light through the window and thought it looked very pretty. But when Pekka bent down to get behind the bath-house door, it was all dark again in the yard, and instead of the *päre* we saw only the lamp mirroring itself in the dark window-panes.

Henceforth we never burnt a *päre* in the dwelling room again. The lamp shone victoriously from the roof, and on Sunday evenings all the townsfolk often used to come to look upon and admire it. It was known all over the parish that our house was the first, after the parsonage, where the lamp had been used. After we had set the example, the magistrate bought a lamp like ours, but as he had never learnt to light it, he was glad to sell it to the inn-keeper, and the innkeeper has it still.

The poorer farmfolk, however, have not been able to get themselves lamps, but even now they do their long evening's work by the glare of a *päre*.

But when we had had the lamp

a short time, father planed the walls
of the dwelling room all smooth and
white, and they never got black
again, especially after the old stove,
which used to smoke, had to make
room for another which discharged
its smoke outside and had a cowl.

Pekka made a new fireplace in
the bath-house out of the stones of
the old stove, and the crickets
flitted thither with the stones—at
least their chirping was never
heard any more in the dwelling
room. Father didn't care a bit,
but we children felt, now and
then, during the long winter
evenings, a strange sort of yearn-
ing after old times, so we very often
found our way down to the bath-
house to listen to the crickets, and
there was Pekka sitting out the
long evenings by the light of his
päre.

PIONEERS.

THEY were both in service at the parsonage, he as stable-boy, she as house-maid. He drove the horses, and she was busy about the house. At meal-times, when they sat each at a corner of the table, they joked together sometimes, but usually they were quarrelling. Their master and mistress thought them a singularly ill-assorted couple : in fact, just like cat and dog, people said.

But, what with fishing-parties at night, what with helping each other at hay-making and corn-cutting by day, the thought of starting a home together gradually grew strong within them. Far away out in the wilderness they had fixed upon a plot for their cottage, by the side of a marsh. There was forest-land and to spare ; it only wanted clearing. The vast, alder-grown flat could be turned into arable land, and meadow-land could be made out of the low-lying ground on both sides of the brook. If only the hut could be built! But wages were low, and one needed a horse and cow at least to start with. Thus circumstances delayed the marriage. But, in the course of the year, the bonds between them were knit still closer, and their prospects for the future grew brighter every day. They spent their leisure hours in totting up what their savings already amounted to, and in estimating how long they must still wait till the indispensably necessary sum had been scraped together. Nobody dreamed that an eager longing after freedom and a burning desire to keep house on their own account were gradually waxing and waxing in this boy and girl. For they had such a nice easy time of it at the parsonage, no cares at all, and food and clothing found. But their hearts were turned towards the wilderness.

Every one was ready with a warning when, one summer, they both refused to continue in service.

" Over yonder the frost rules and rages, and you'll only load yourselves with debt. A family soon grows up, and we've quite enough of beggars already." But they had thought and worked the matter out for the last five years, and their minds were made up. The priest had to put up the banns for them, and in the autumn they quitted his house.

The following winter they were still living in lodgings. Ville however, was busy with the building of his hut and did a day's work at the parsonage at odd times, and Anni helped the priest's wife with sewing and weaving.

The wedding was celebrated at the Whitsuntide following. The cost of it was paid by the parsonage people, and the vicar himself married his former servants in the large room of the parsonage. But when the married couple had taken their leave and the priest, standing at the window, saw them disappearing down the path, he shook his head anxiously, and said, " Let the young people try what they can make of it, but the wilderness is not to be cleared away by the capital of a boy and girl."

Finland's wilderness had, however, been cleared by such capital,
and yet the vicar was right too.

We, the youths of the parish,
escorted our dear old friends to
their new home. The long summer
day passed away as we wandered
through the forest bright with
vernal green, and **we** danced away
the night in the new hut. The
planks **of the new** dwelling were
still quite roughish ; the jagged,
unsawn timber ends jutted unevenly
out of the knots in the wood and
the brown river appeared to be
spreading everywhere over the
newly reclaimed field. But on the
hill-slope the fresh rye shoots glis-
tened bright and green amidst the
sooty tree-stumps, and on the plot
of land cleared for corn the trees
were lopped gaunt and dry. The
young hostess lit a bonfire on the
clearing and milked her cow there
for the first time. Ville and I sat
on a stone and watched her bustling
about in the sickly sheen of the
evening sun : she still wore her
bridal garments.

Ville had no **doubt** whatever of
success.

" If only we keep our health and
the frost doesn't come "—and as if

anticipating my thoughts, he added, "I know that the swamp down there is a regular nest of frost, but if a fellow always keeps his arms a-going, I'll drive the forest further away and open up a place for the sun, and then . . . It still feels a little chilly here of an evening perhaps, but come here next summer and have a look at us then."

I paid them no visit next summer or the summer after that either. I must confess that I clean forgot them ; but once, when I was at home, I asked how they were getting on.

"They have been obliged to get into debt," was my father's answer.

"And Anni has been ailing," added my mother.

Some years had passed. I was now a student, and had a gun and a retriever, and was passing my autumn vacation in the country.

One dull October day I was wandering about the woods and hit. upon a narrow path which seemed familiar to me. It began to drizzle ; the dog was scampering on in front. Suddenly he began to growl and then to bark fiercely. We heard in front of us the tramp

of a horse. Presently, at a turn of
the road, the horse became visible ;
it was harnessed between a pair of
shafts the ends of which dragged
upon the ground. A white cloth
hung upon the collar-trees, and
right across the shafts lay a fastened-
down coffin. Behind the car
tramped Ville, like a plougher
after his plough. He had quite
enough to do to keep his load in
equilibrium.

He looked worn out : his cheeks
were pale, his eyes dim and
faded.

It was only when he heard my
name that he recognised me.

"But what sort of a load have
you got there ?" said I.

"My dead wife," was the reply.

"Dead ?"

"Yes, she is dead."

By a little questioning I learnt
their brief, predicted story : frost,
debt, many children, his wife sick,
and at last dead from overwork.
Now he had to carry her to the
grave, but the roads were so very
bad. He only hoped that the
coffin might hold out till he
reached the church. He tweaked
at the reins for the horse had over-
stepped the path and was searching

for a little grass among the withered leaves. " Wo-ho ! "

It was trying to satisfy its hunger. The beast was in just as wretched a state as the man : it looked like a skeleton.

Ville took leave of me and went on his way without lifting his eyes from his load. The shaft-poles cut two parallel furrows in the sandy path.

I went in the opposite direction and came to a marsh where they had begun to dig a draining ditch but stopped short when the work was only half done. The path, familiar to me since the bridal tour, led to the little hut.

Behind the fence a lean cow was lowing feebly and a pig was grunting in the plot of yard, the wicket-gate of which had been left open. In the middle of the yard stood an empty bed, and the dead woman's bedclothes had been cast upon the fence. The jagged timber-ends still stuck up out of the knots in the wood of which the hut was built. In the frame of the window, the panes of which were dim and dirty, stood a withering balsam in a little birch-wood box.

The man had succeeded, however,

in clearing out a little bit of the
wilderness. A small strip of corn-
land of about a couple of acres in
width and about half as much land
dug up for sowing formed an open-
ing in the forest. But at this point
his powers seemed to have broken
down. The birch-wood he had
felled and the alder-groves he had
changed into meadows. But behind them stood the dark pine
forest like an insurmountable wall.
There he had been obliged to stop
short.

I stood for a long time in the
yard of the deserted cottage. The
wind whined fiercely in the forest,
and called forth from the mouth of
my gun-barrel, which lay close to
my ear, a mournful wailing sound.

    *   *   *   *   *

The first pioneer has fulfilled his
task ; the man can do no more good
there now. His strength, his energy
are gone, the fire of his eye is ex-
tinguished and the self-confidence
of his marriage morn has forsaken
him.

Another will certainly come after
him and take over the cottage plot.
He perhaps will have better luck.
But he will have a lighter task to
begin with, for before him no longer

stands the savage forest quite un-
touched by man. He can settle
down into a ready-made hut, and
sow in the plot of land which
another has ploughed up before
him. That cottage plot will, no
doubt, become a large and wealthy
farm, and in course of time a village
will grow up around it.

Nobody thinks of those who first
dug up the earth with all their
capital, the only capital they pos-
sessed—their youthful energies.
They were merely a simple lad and
lass, and both of them came there
with empty hands.

But it is just with such people's
capital that Finland's wildernesses
have been rooted up and converted
into broad acres. Had these two
only remained at the parsonage, he
as a coachman and she as a house-
maid, then perhaps the course of
their own lives would have been
free enough of care. But the
wilderness would not have been
cultivated, and the foreposts of civi-
lisation would not have been planted
in the midst of the forest.

When the rye blooms and the
ears of corn ripen in our fields, let
us call to mind these first martyrs
of colonisation.

We cannot raise monuments upon their graves, for the tale of them is by thousands, and their names we know not.

LOYAL.

I.

HE had been obliged to pass the summer in town to relieve a well-to-do colleague, who was spending his vacation in the country. He was engaged, but couldn't think of marrying till he had got a fixed income. So he had to push his way.

It was tiresome and trying to be plodding away in Helsingfors during the summer, and it was especially hard immediately after dinner. The forenoon passed away pretty tolerably in official work, but at three o'clock one had to be off to the eating-house, where the sun shone right into the room, where it was hot, where the furniture had unpleasant white coverings, the chan-

delier was enveloped in a cloth,
wretched oil-paintings hung upon
the walls, and where one had neither
the feeling of home nor the comfort
of a tavern.   And from thence one
had to drag one's self off to one's
lodgings in Kronohagen, and go
along streets which the architects
had made half as small again as
they need have been, and past
houses with chalked windows.

It was midsummer—afternoon.
All his colleagues had been invited
to a picnic somewhere on the coast
among the islands. But Antti had
no acquaintances, and so, after
vainly turning over in his mind
what he should do with himself, he
had returned to his lodgings. After
coming home he usually sat with
his elbows resting on the table,
smoking and looking through the
window over to the other side of
the street, where a stone house was
being built. Then he would remove
the pillow from his bed to his sofa,
kick his boots under the table and
go to sleep for an hour or two, or
perhaps a little more. But even
after that a good many hours of the
evening still remained empty. What
was he to do with them, those long
monotonous hours ? The Concert

Room and the restaurants of Bruns-
park and Hesperia were dear, and
besides, it's not quite the thing to
be sitting there *every* evening. Yet,
if he recollected aright, he had sat
there *nearly* every evening, on
Saturday evening because it *was*
Saturday, on Sunday for a similar
reason ; the other days were regular
exceptions.

Regarded from the usual place
behind the table the world to-day
looked more than usually tiresome.
The work-place opposite was also
empty, the door in the scaffolding
was locked, and there was " no ad-
mittance except on business."

To be in the country now, far
away in Savolax, at home with his
beloved ! What rapture ! To lie
at his ease in the hammock, row,
sail, wander hand in hand, sit in
her lap and make her sit in his, to
kiss and caress when nobody was
looking !

He began thinking what he should
set about doing, and resolved to
write a letter. He took out pen
and paper, placed them in front of
him, and jotted down the date in
the upper corner, and a little below
it " Dearest Mia " ! But as he was
not quite clear with what he should

begin and how he should go on, he
resolved to first of all sleep off a bit
of his midday heaviness.

When, after getting up again, he
again sat down in front of his writing-paper, where the lately written
words were dry and shiny, he didn't
feel in the humour for writing even
now. He lit a cigarette, but even
that did not give him inspiration.
There was absolutely nothing to
write about. Everybody who, like
Antti, has been engaged for three
years will know that a subject is often
lacking under such circumstances.
One ought to give expression to
one's love and interpret one's
thoughts, but one cannot hit upon
fresh words. Antti had already
used all the suitable phrases he
knew of in the language, besides in-
venting not a few brand-new ones.

He was obliged to get up and
walk up and down the floor, he
drank some water, opened the window and leaned out of it. As far as
his eye could reach, all the streets
were as empty as his own thoughts.
Everybody must certainly have
gone to the country. It was seven
o'clock. By this time they were all
picnicing at Hogholm or Degerö or
Fölisö.

He rallied all his energies and succeeded in putting down on his writing-paper : " It is now mid-summer afternoon, and I am sitting alone in my room and writing to you. If you only knew how I . . ." But here he stopped short, he suddenly felt himself quite used up, he could no more get along with it than when as a schoolboy he had been obliged to write essays on subjects he didn't understand.

While he was staring at his finger-nails, he heard in the street below the rapid steps and jerky talk of people who are in a violent hurry. Two pretty girls were hastening down to the sea-shore. They had presumably got leave to be out for the whole night. They had their best clothes on, white hoods with long fringes, and clothes which fitted closely to their supple and vigorous shapes.

Antti fell a-thinking that for three years he had been faithful to his sweetheart, and vanquished like a man all the temptations which had come in his way. . . . The girls swung rapidly round the corner, and the street was as empty as before. Antti's thoughts were also empty.

" But why can't I go too ? Why

can't I share in the popular fes-
tivities at Degerö, whither the steamboat goes every half-hour? Such a
splendid evening as it is, too! I swallow dust all the week through, and
when, for once in a way, the opportunity of flying to Nature's bosom
presents itself, I lock myself up in
my room!"

He stretched himself, puffed the
air out of his lungs and tapped himself in the ribs. He felt quite a
stitch in the side from too much
sitting down.

There was one impediment, however. It was mail-day, and he
would miss the post if he postponed
writing his letter now. Mia will
certainly walk the whole of the two
miles to the post-office, and if she
finds nothing there, she will be un-
happy and accuse him of coldness,
and then there will be long explana-
tions and reassurances. But then,
at any rate, one would have something to write about afterwards.
Besides, when one returns from a
little pleasure trip, one can always
manage to scrape together news
enough to fill a sheet. But it is of
no very great consequence. A fellow doesn't always feel in the
humour to write love-letters. If

she is offended she must get pleased
again, that's all!

If Antti had only been able to
search his own heart he would have
discovered that this very same frame
of mind, an almost unconscious im-
patience, had revealed itself within
him once or twice before. That
very winter, when his sweetheart
was in town, and they were constantly together, a sort of inertia, a
sort of unwillingness to give free
play to his feelings, had come over
him. He could not throw into his
voice the tenderness he wished to
show, and it was only now and then
at the *soirées* of the " Finnish Literary Society," when she had a new
dress on, or when he had become a
little warmed up by refreshments,
that he could still wax enthusiastic,
as he had done during the earlier
days of his engagement, and so make
heart and voice vibrate in unison.

He stuck the letter he had begun
into his drawer, hastily dressed himself, filled his cigar-case with cigarettes, stuffed a box of matches into
his pocket, and sprang rapidly down
the stairs as if he were afraid of
being too late. When one looked
at him from behind as he hurried
along, he gave one the idea of a

man who was about to do something
which he felt was not quite right.

In a few moments he was standing
by the side of a steamboat at the
South Haven, and watching the
pleasure-seekers stepping on board.
Carters, whose horse-collars were
covered with birch-leaves in honour
of Midsummer Day, drove, one after
the other, through the market-place
down to the strand. Groups of men
with flowers in their hats, and
women with roses in their breasts,
were hastening down to the steamboat with their wraps across their
arms.

The steamboat was bright with
flags from stem to stern, and midsummer birch boughs covered the
railings of the deck. Antti also had
bought a little bouquet from a
flower-girl.

They are all hastening out into
the country. They are all hastening
on board along the landing-stage.
Antti still hesitates. But just when
they are about to unloose the ropes,
he skips on board too.

II.

BUT why does he sit so disconso-
lately there on a stone by the way-

side a little distance from the
pleasure-ground whence the sounds
of music and a merry hum proceed
incessantly ? Why does he long to
be away from all this merry-making
the very moment he has got there,
and only awaits another steamboat
to take him back to town ?

When a cat has pounced down
upon a flock of chickens without
success, she sneaks shamefacedly
away with her tail between her legs,
and vexation in her heart.

Antti was convinced within himself that he had meant to pounce
upon nothing, but, for all that, he
had turned aside hither, sullen and
depressed, and was now prodding
about in the sand with his cane.

The girls from the steamboat had
skipped down upon the bridge.
They were unusually free and light-
some in their movements, and their
kirtles rustled all about them. Young
men came forward to meet them,
nonchalantly took them round their
waists or under their arms, and,
without more ado, swung them round
once or twice before they let them
go. In a long stream, which filled
the whole road, they then hastened
towards the pleasure-ground, frisk-
ing and bouncing as they went.

Antti went slowly forward, though
there was a slight tickling sensation
in the soles of his feet, and he let
those who were in a hurry pass him
by.   One petticoat after another
whisked past him.   The lasses pretended to fly from the lads who
pelted after them.   But they soon
allowed themselves to be caught,
and, hand in hand, they reached the
pleasure place.

When Antti came up the dancing
was in full swing.   The musicians
stood in the centre.   The sport was
fast and furious.   The dancers held
tightly to each other all through ;
they took big steps and long hops,
their movements were brisk, and
they swung rapidly round and round.
Hoods shrunk down upon shoulders,
and hats over necks, and here and
there a cigar could be seen stuck
nonchalantly in the corner of a
mouth.

There were soldiers there, broad-
chested sailors, sturdy peasants from
the islands, artisans, and a few
students in broad-brimmed hats.
The women were shop-girls, milli-
ners, tobacconist nymphs, artisans'
daughters, and servant-girls.   Antti
knew one or two of them by sight,
and a few of them by name.   But

nobody knew him. For it was a long time since he had made one of them.

And not a soul there troubles itself about him. For every one there has her own young man, nay, there are some of the lads who have a sweetheart under each arm. Antti has nothing but his stick on which he leans now and then, while he glances from one group to the other. Mia is, somehow or other, far, far away. The women here are, in his opinion, quite pretty. Amongst the mob there were some so young, so smart, and so fresh, that it was delightful to look at them. There was something so fresh about them, something so naïve, something of the artless joy of young calves. They are now celebrating their midsummer fête; they have the whole night before them; their masters and mistresses are all in the country, and they have resolved, for once in the year, to revel on the island, on the green meadow, among the rocks and trees.

What on earth were they laughing at? Whatever could they find to amuse them in the dull witticisms of their gallants? Antti could not for the life of him make it out. But

he would very much have liked to
have been just such a belauded hero
in their estimation. He also would
have liked to clip them round the
neck, whisper some such tickling
jest in their ears, learn all their little
ways, and for that evening, at any
rate, appropriate to himself those
half-shamefaced confidences to which
girls abandon themselves so readily.

For a long time he stood lurking
there with stiff, darkened looks,
stolid features, and a load upon his
heart.

Suppose now he were to join the
group and partake of its pastimes?
Nobody there knew him. What
harm could it do to anybody? And
how was any one the better for the
life he was living now? *Living*,
indeed! It was not living; it was
withering! The cowardly idealism
of these latter days is regular non-
sense, or, any rate, sheer childish-
ness. Yes, cowardly, and nothing
else. People don't dare to live now
as Nature bids them. It is an
eternal avoiding opportunities and
balancing chances. Not one in a
hundred is really loyal at heart.
Now look at those people there!
Their life is something quite different. They know nothing about

the silly prejudices of educated
people. They all enjoy life in its
fulness, the women as well as the
men. That is why they are all so
fresh, gay, and lively. They know
how to celebrate their midsummer
fête, and rejoice in the feast of the
sun.

Thus spoke his thoughts, and his
eyes followed a fresh and lovely girl
who is standing there bareheaded,
fanning her burning cheeks with
her handkerchief. He plucked up
courage and drew near to her. He
asks how the young lady is, and
remarks that it is fine weather. He
tries to be free and easy, but his
voice strikes him as hollow and
affected. The girl replies as if he
were a perfect stranger, nay, almost
with awe.

When Antti asks her if she will
have a dance, she answers, " Yes ! "
but discreetly, solemnly, just as if
she were a fashionable young lady,
and with nothing at all of that
frank abandonment with which
Antti saw her skip just now towards another cavalier who was
coming to her with an invitation.
During the dance Antti pulled her
towards him, and pressed her hand,
but without meeting with any

response. He knows that they do
not go well together—don't get
along at all, somehow. Whenever
he tries to put some go into it and
swings her round, they get out of
step and have to stop and begin all
over again. When the dance is
over they stand for some time side
by side without speaking a word.

" May I offer you some tea ? "
asks Antti at last.

"No, thank you; it is warm
enough without that."

" Perhaps you would like a little
lemonade, or something of that
sort ? "

" Nothing, thank you."

"Are you looking out for any
acquaintance, Miss ? "

" Acquaintance ? What do you
mean ? "

"Why, because Miss, you seem
to be peeping about so."

" No ; I have no particular acquaintance."

" Then are you quite alone here,
Miss ? "

To this Antti got no answer at
all.

" Do you intend to stay here long,
Miss ? "

" I don't think of leaving just
yet."

"Wouldn't you like a little walk? It is certainly very pretty in the woods over there."

"One can walk at any time. I have come here to dance."

"The dance is just over."

The same instant up came a young artisan swell in a white waistcoat, and took the girl to dance. They treated each other as equals. They whirled now to the right and now to the left, and laughed good-naturedly whenever any one bumped against them.

Antti followed them with his eyes. He waited for them to separate, but when the music ceased they went off for a walk with their arms round each other's waists. All the other couples did the same thing, and soon the whole wood was swarming with people. Every hill-slope was alive with them, and there was a laughing, and a whispering, and a giggling at the foot of every tree.

And so that is why Antti sits there so downcast and almost devout, prodding about in the sand with his stick, and with more than half a mind to go home.

It seems to him that he is somewhat superfluous here, and he feels

that he has not been a success. The
world is such a meaningless blank
to him now ; life tastes like mouldy
wood which does not taste of anything at all.

He is quite nauseated by the
dance-music, which has now begun
again, and by the noise in the
pleasure-ground also. When such-
like folks set to dancing, they hop
about like so many calves. It is
really, after all, a very rough-and-
tumble business.

He feels the want of Mia. A
longing after love suddenly over-
comes him, and he is seized with an
irresistible desire to write to her,
right tenderly and affectionately.

Had he been disloyal? In thought,
perhaps. But the fact that he is
ready to be off with the very first
steamboat proves that he is man
enough to overcome temptation and
has a will of his own.

III.

No sooner did he get into his room
than he took from the drawer the
letter he had already begun :—

"DEAREST MIA,—It is now Midsummer afternoon, and I am sitting

alone in my room and writing to
you. If you only knew how I——"
—here begins the continuation,
which ran on now quite easily—
" love you beyond everything. You
have no idea how I long for you,
how I regard the prospect of one
day possessing you as my highest
bliss. Why are you not here that
I might say it to you by word of
mouth, and whisper it in your ear ?
Why can I not press you to my
breast, kiss your forehead, your red
cheeks, your rosy lips, caress you,
and throw my arms round your
neck ?

" Without you I am nothing ! I
thought I would amuse myself a
little to-day, so I joined a popular
pleasure party at Degerö. But I
very soon came back again—came
back again full of grief and longing.
I couldn't get on at all in such
society. Perhaps I am a little too
aristocratic ; but, anyway, I feel
almost a physical repulsion when I
think of how it was there and what
I saw. Nothing is so unbeautiful,
I think, as when a half-fuddled mob
of that sort from town is let loose
in the country in the midst of lovely
scenery. I was glad to withdraw
from it as quickly as possible. As

soon as ever I had drunk a cup of
tea, I took the first boat and came
straight to town.

"Yet I don't at all repent that I
went there, for on the way back I
began to feel so lonely, so disturbed,
my thoughts were of you alone, my
own Mia. If I were a poet, if I
had the pencil of a painter, what a
picture would I not draw of my
frame of mind, and what a splendid
description I would give of the
scenery I saw and admired from the
deck of the steamboat. In the front
of our steamboat, *The Nixey*, the
water foamed and frothed as we
passed through the eastern rocky
channel. The sea was as still as the
forest along the shore. The islands
and the sound lay so lovely there
in the clearness of the midsummer
night. On the shore burned the
bonfires, and here and there one
could hear songs and music. What
a delicious voyage ! But how many
hundreds of times more splendid
and more beautiful it would have
been if you, my own Mia, had been
sitting beside me !

"But although you were not
actually present, you were nevertheless with me in spirit. I thought
of you the whole time. I conjured

up our own pretty little house
which we will make for ourselves
when I get regular employment.
We will live simply for each other,
we will choose our own society, we
will only invite some of our best
friends.

"Do you love me, Mia, as you
used to do? Such strange thoughts
are borne in upon me sometimes.
I wonder whether you love me now
as you loved me when we were first
engaged. I am sometimes jealous
of the whole world, and fancy that
nobody cares about me—not even
you. You are forgetting me, perhaps, in the country yonder, where
there are so many young people.
Forgive me these doubts, which I
only mention to you because I
promised to be candid. I know
that it is all imagination, that not
even in thought could you be disloyal to me ; but I feel like this
because I am so lonely here, so forsaken by everybody. It would make
me so happy to hear that I am
mistaken. Say that you love me—
I know you *do*—but I implore you
to tell me so, and repeat it a
thousand times.

"Oh, how delightful it really is to
know that there is somebody whom

one loves and who loves one in
return, to whom one can tell all
one's sorrows and open one's heart
and one's whole soul !

" Farewell, my own dear, beloved
Mia ! Write me a long letter—
write about everything you think
and feel. Every stroke written by
your hand, every word uttered by
your lips, is dearer to me than gold.
What is all earthly gold compared
with " — Antti paused for a moment to reflect how he should go
on, but the same instant a happy
thought occurred to him, and he
added—"our good fortune in having discovered one another's hearts?

" My love to Aunt and Uncle.
A thousand ardent kisses from your
eternally loyal

"ANTTI.

" P.S.—I haven't said half I want
to say yet, but I must carry this
letter to the railway this very night.
I will put it in the post-box at the
station, lest it go astray, and you
pay a visit to the post-office in vain.
When I come home again and lay
me down to sleep, my last thought
before I close my eyes will be—
yourself.—Ever thine."

Such a tender, affectionate letter Mia had not received from Antti for a long time. She who knew of nothing else, who thought of nothing else but Antti, she who believed that no other man was so upright, so pure, so noble—for she knew all about his views on all subjects—she was so glad when she received this fresh proof of her sweetheart's love that she locked herself in her own room straightway, and wrote him this letter :—

She began : " Dearest, dearest, dearest Antti ! " And then she said that she was still all of a tremble with rapture at the thought that he loved her so intensely. She had read through his letter again and again, and when she went to sleep, she meant to lay it under her pillow. She had cried when she thought how lonely Antti must be in that nasty Helsingfors. Alas ! if only she could do something to hasten on the founding of their own little home ! "How *could* you imagine, Antti, that I would ever be disloyal to you? I think of nothing else, I care for nothing else but you, only you. I take no part in the pastimes of the young people here, as you may suppose, except very, very seldom. And if you only wish it, I will see no society at all, nor go any excursions, nor accept any invitations, just as you do not dance nor take any pleasure in popular amusements. Often I sit in the garden beneath the birch-tree in which your name is carved and in whose shadow we spent so many unforgettable moments last summer. I sit and sew, and hum the songs you love. Sometimes I put out the boat, and row out upon the lake. How lovely it is there! But you have indeed become a poet. Again and again I have read your fine description of the steamboat journey along the rocky coast. I read it out to papa and mamma too. You are not angry, are you? They think so much of you, and always ask me what you write about."

Mia wrote and wrote sheet after sheet. She was "so happy, so happy." She had been wrong in doubting Antti's feelings and thinking that he was growing cold. Her conscience almost reproached her for having been able to think so ill of her own loyal Antti. And she concluded her letter like this: "Oh, oh, how *frightfully* much I

love you! Farewell, dearest, most
beloved Antti. I send you thousands and thousands of kisses.—Thy
little MIA."